BEFORE

(A MACKENZIE WHITE M̶y̶s̶t̶e̶r̶y̶

BLAKE PIERCE

ISBN: 978-1-63291-846-8

BOOKS BY BLAKE PIERCE

RILEY PAIGE MYSTERY SERIES
ONCE GONE (Book #1)
ONCE TAKEN (Book #2)
ONCE CRAVED (Book #3)
ONCE LURED (Book #4)

MACKENZIE WHITE MYSTERY SERIES
BEFORE HE KILLS (Book #1)
BEFORE HE SEES (Book #2)

AVERY BLACK MYSTERY SERIES
CAUSE TO KILL (Book #1)
CAUSE TO RUN (Book #2)

PROLOGUE

Susan Kellerman understood the need to dress nicely. She was representing her company and trying to win over new buyers, so her appearance went a long way. What she did not understand, though, was why in God's name she had to wear heels. She was wearing a pretty summer dress and had the perfect pair of flats to go with it. But no…corporate insisted on heels. Something about sophistication.

I doubt heels have anything to do with acquiring a sale, she thought. Especially not if the would-be client is a man. According to her sell -sheet, the person in the house she was currently approaching *was* a man. Given that, Susan checked the collar of her dress. She was showing *some* cleavage but nothing scandalous.

That, she thought, *shows sophistication.*

With her rather large and cumbersome display case in hand, she clomped up the steps in her heels and rang the doorbell. As she waited, she took a quick glance around the front of the house. It was a basic little house situated on the outskirts of a middle-class neighborhood. The grass had been recently cut, but the small flower beds bordering the tiny set of stairs to the front door were badly in need of weeding.

It was a quiet neighborhood, but not the kind Susan would live in. The houses were one-story little saltboxes splattered along the streets. Most, she assumed, were owned by older couples or those struggling to pay their bills. This house in particular looked about one strong storm or financial crisis away from becoming the property of the bank.

She reached out to ring the bell again but the door was answered before she could touch it. The man that answered was of average size and build. She guessed him to be about forty or so. There was something feminine about him, something she could see from the way he simply answered the door and gave her a wide, bright smile.

"Good morning," the man said.

"Good morning," she said.

She knew his name but had been instructed by those that trained her to never use it until the lines of communication were wide open. When you greeted them by name right away, it made them feel like targets rather than customers—even when they had scheduled the appointment ahead of time.

1

Not wanting to allow him a moment to ask her questions and therefore take control of the conversation, she added: "I was wondering if you might have a moment to speak with me about your current diet."

"Diet?" the man asked with a smirk. "I'm not on much of a diet. I sort of eat what I want."

"Oh, that must be nice," Susan said, putting on her best charming smile and chipper tone of voice. "As I'm sure you know, not many people over the age of thirty can say that and maintain a healthy body type."

For the first time, the man looked at the case in her left hand. He smiled again and this time it was a lazy one—the sort of smile someone might flash when they know they've been had.

"So what are you selling?"

It was a sarcastic comment, but at least it wasn't a door closing in her face. She took that as the first victory toward getting inside. "Well, I'm here on behalf of A Better You University," she said. "We offer adults over the age of thirty a very easy and methodical way to stay in shape without hitting the gym or altering their lifestyle too much."

The man sighed and his hand went to the door. He looked bored, ready to send her packing. "And how do you do that?"

"Through a combination of protein shakes made with our very own protein powders and more than fifty healthy recipes to give your daily nutrition the boost it needs."

"And that's it?"

"That's it," she said.

The man considered it for a moment, looking to Susan and then to the large pack in her hands. He then looked at his watch and gave a shrug.

"I'll tell you what," he said. "I have to leave in ten minutes. If you can convince me in that amount of time, you've got a customer. Anything to keep me from going back to the gym."

"Splendid," Susan said, cringing internally at the fake cheer in her voice.

The man stepped aside and waved her into the house. "Come on in," he said.

She stepped inside and entered a small living room. An ancient-looking television sat on a scarred entertainment center. A few dusty old chairs sat in the corners of the room along with a crumpled sofa. There were ceramic figurines and doilies everywhere. It looked more like some old woman's house than a forty-something single man's.

For reasons she did not know, she heard internal alarms going off. But then she tried to thwart her fear with shaky logic. *So he's either incredibly off or this isn't his house. Maybe he lives with his mother.*

"Is here okay?" she asked, pointing to the coffee table in front of the couch.

"Yes, right there is fine," the man said. He smiled at her as he closed the door.

The moment the door was closed, Susan felt something stir in her gut. It felt like the room had grown cold and all of her senses were responding to it. Something was wrong. It was a bizarre feeling. She looked at the nearest ceramic figure—a little boy pulling a wagon—as if for some sort of answer.

She busied herself by opening up her case. She took out a few packs of the A Better You University Protein Powder and the complimentary mini-blender (a retail value of $35 but yours absolutely free with your first purchase!) to distract herself.

"Now," she said, trying to remain calm and ignore the chill she still felt. "Are you more interested in weight loss, weight gain, or maintaining your current body type?"

"I'm not sure," the man said, standing over the coffee table and looking at the goods. "What would you say?"

Susan found it hard to talk. She felt scared now and for no real reason.

She looked over at the door. Her heart thumped in her chest. Had he *locked* the door when he closed it? She couldn't tell from where she sat.

She then realized that the man was still waiting for a response. She shook the cobwebs away and tried to slip back into presenter mode.

"Well, I don't know," she said.

She wanted to look to the door again. Suddenly the fake eyes of every porcelain figure in the room seemed to be staring at her— leering at her like a predator.

"I don't eat *too* bad," the man said. "But I do have a soft spot for key lime pie. Would I still be able to eat key lime pie on your program?"

"Possibly," she said. She sifted through her materials, pulling the case closer to her. *Ten minutes,* she thought, getting more and more uneasy with the passing of each second. *He said he had ten minutes. I can make it that long.*

She found the small pamphlet that showed what the man would be able to eat on the program and looked up to him to hand it over.

3

He took it and when he did, his hand brushed hers for just a moment.

Again, alarms sounded in her head. She had to get out of there. She'd never had such a reaction from stepping into a potential client's house but this was so overpowering that it was all she could think about.

"I'm sorry," she said, gathering the case and her materials back up. "But I just now remembered that I have a meeting to attend in less than an hour, and it's all the way on the other side of town."

"Oh," he said, looking at the pamphlet she had just handed him. "Well, I understand. Sure. I hope you can make it on time."

"Thanks," she said quickly.

He offered her the pamphlet and she took it with a trembling hand. She put it into the case and started for the front door.

It *was* locked.

"Excuse me," the man said.

Susan turned, still reaching for the doorknob.

She barely saw the punch coming. All she saw was a blinding white fist as it slammed into her mouth. She felt blood flowing right away and tasted it on her tongue. She fell directly back onto the couch.

She opened her mouth to scream and felt like the right side of her jaw was locked up. As she tried getting to her feet, the man was there again, this time driving a knee into her stomach. The wind rushed out of her and she could do nothing but curl up, fighting for breath. As she did, she was dimly aware of the man picking her up and throwing her over his shoulder as if she was some helpless cavewoman that he was dragging back to his cave.

She tried fighting against him, but she still could not draw any breath into her lungs. It was like being paralyzed, like drowning. Her whole body felt limp, including her head. She was dripping blood onto the back of the man's shirt and this was all she saw as he took her through the house.

At some point, she realized that he had taken her into another house—a house that was somehow attached to the one she had been in just moments ago. She was dropped to the floor like a sack of rocks, striking her head on a scarred linoleum floor. Bright dots of pain flared across her eyes as she was finally able to take in the smallest of breaths. She rolled over but when she managed to get to her feet, he was there again.

Her eyes were growing hazy but she could make out enough to see that he had opened some sort of small door in the side of a wall—hidden behind some sort of false paneling. It was dark in

4

there, layered with dust and some sort of puffy insulation that hung down in torn tatters. Her heart slammed against her chest as if trying to break through her breastbone when she realized that he was taking her in there.

"You'll be safe here," the man told her as he hunched over and dragged her into the crawlspace.

She found herself in the dark, lying down on stiff boards that served as the floor. All she could smell was dust and her own blood, still trickling from her busted nose. The man…she knew his name but could not recall it. The word was blood and pain and a tight pain in her chest as she still fought for breath.

She finally drew one in and wanted to use it to scream. But instead, she let it fill her lungs, relieving her body. In that moment of brief relief, she heard the crawlspace door close somewhere behind her and then she was stranded in the darkness.

The last thing she heard before her world went black was his laughter, just outside the door.

"Don't worry," he said. "This will all be over soon."

CHAPTER ONE

The rain was coming down steadily, just hard enough so that Mackenzie White could not hear her own footfalls. This was good. It meant that the man she was chasing down would not be able to hear them, either.

Still, she had to advance with caution. Not only was it raining, but it was late at night. The suspect could easily use the darkness to his advantage just like she could. And the weak flickering streetlights were doing her no favors.

With her hair nearly soaked and her rain coat so wet that it was basically plastered to her, Mackenzie crossed the deserted street in a near march. Ahead of her, her partner was already at the targeted building. She could see his shape crouching low by the side of the old concrete structure. As she neared him, illuminated only by the moonlight and a single streetlight a block away, she tightened her slick grip on the Academy-issued Glock she carried in her hands.

She was starting to like the feel of a gun in her hands. It was more than a sense of security but something closer to a relationship. When she held a gun in her hands and knew that she was going to shoot it, she felt an intimate connection to it. She had never felt this while working as an underappreciated detective in Nebraska; it was something new that the FBI Academy had chiseled out of her.

She reached the building and huddled up along the side of it with her partner. Here, at least, the rain was no longer pelting her.

Her partner's name was Harry Dougan. He was twenty-two, well-built, and cocky in a subtle and almost respectable way. She was relieved to see that he looked a little unnerved, too.

"Did you get a visual?" Mackenzie asked him.

"No. But the front room is clear. You can see that much through the window," he said, pointing ahead of them. There was a single window there, broken and jagged.

"How many rooms?" she asked.

"Three that I know of for sure."

"Let me lead," she said. She made sure it did not sound like a question. Even here in Quantico, women had to be assertive to be taken seriously.

He gestured for her to go ahead. As she dashed in front of him, she slid to the front of the building. She peered around and saw that the coast was clear. These streets were eerily empty and everything looked dead.

She gave a quick motion for Harry to come forward and he did without hesitation. He was holding his own Glock steady in his hands, holding it low to the ground in their pursuit, just like they had been trained to do. Together, they crept toward the front door of the building. It was an abandoned concrete slab of a place—maybe an old warehouse or storage place—and the door showed its age. It also made it obvious that it was open, a dark crack revealing a sliver of the building's interior.

Mackenzie looked at Harry and counted down with her fingers. *Three, two…one!*

She pressed her back tight against the concrete wall as Harry went low, pushed the door open, and strafed inside. She wheeled in behind him, the two of them operating like a well-oiled machine. However, once inside the building, there was almost no light. She quickly went for her flashlight at her side. Just as she was about to click it on, she stopped herself. A flashlight beam would be a dead giveaway for their location. The suspect would see them far in advance and could likely escape them…again.

She replaced the flashlight and reclaimed the lead again, creeping in front of Harry with the Glock now trained ahead to the door on her right. As her eyes adjusted to the darkness, she could see more details of the place. It was mostly barren. A few soggy cardboard boxes were pressed against a far wall. A sawhorse and several old cables lay discarded near the back corner of the room. Other than that, the central room was empty.

Mackenzie walked toward the door to her right. It was really just a doorway, the actual door having long been removed. Inside, shadows concealed nearly everything. Other than a broken glass bottle and what looked to be several rat droppings, the room was empty.

She stopped and started to turn around when she realized that Harry was following far too close behind her. She nearly stepped on his feet as she backed away from the room.

"Sorry," he whispered in the dark. "I thought it—"

He was cut off by the sound of a gunshot. This was instantly followed by an *oof* noise from Harry's mouth as he went to the ground.

Mackenzie pressed hard against the wall as another blast came. The shot pounded the wall from the other side; she could feel the impact of it against her back.

She knew that if she acted quickly, she could take the perp down right now rather than engaging in a shootout from around the wall. She looked at Harry, saw that he was still moving and coherent for the most part, and reached out to him. She hauled him through the doorway, out of the line of fire. When she did, another shot came. She felt it go just over her shoulder, the air whizzing around her raincoat.

When she had Harry to safety, she wasted no time and decided to act. She grabbed her flashlight, clicked it on, and tossed it out the door. It clattered on the ground seconds later, its white beam dancing wildly along the floor on the other side of the wall.

Following the clattering noise, Mackenzie whirled her body out of the doorway. She was crouched low, her hands skimming the floor as she curled herself into a quick, tight roll. As she rolled hard to the left, she saw the shape of the perp directly to her right, still focused on the flashlight.

Coming out of her roll, she extended her right leg with a vicious amount of force. It caught the perp on the backside of the leg, just below the knee. The suspect buckled a bit and that was all she needed. She sprang up and wrapped her right arm around his neck as he sagged and brought him hard to the ground. With a knee to the solar plexus and a deft motion with her left arm, the perp was down, trapped, and quickly disarmed as his rifle went to the floor.

From somewhere else within the old building, a loud voice said, *"Halt!"*

A series of bright white bulbs popped on with audible clicks, flooding the building in light.

Mackenzie stood up and looked down to the suspect. He was smiling up at her. It was a familiar face—one she had seen in her training modules several times, usually barking orders and instructions at the agent trainees.

She held her hand out and he took it from his place on the floor. "Damn good work, White."

"Thank you," she said.

From behind her, Harry stumbled forward, holding his stomach. "Are we absolutely certain they're just packing bean bags in those things?" he asked.

"Not only that, but these are low-grade," the instructor said. "Next time we'll use the riot bags."

"Awesome," Harry grunted.

A few people started filing into the room as the Hogan's Alley run came to an end. It was Mackenzie's third session in the Alley, a mock-up of a derelict street that was heavily used by the FBI in training agent trainees for real-world situations.

While two instructors stood by Harry, letting him know what he had done wrong and how he could have prevented being shot, another instructor headed directly over to Mackenzie. His name was Simon Lee, an older man that looked like life had dealt him a crap hand and he had responded by beating the hell out of it.

"Amazing work, Agent White," he said. "That roll was so damn fast that I barely saw it. Still…it was a little reckless. If there had been more than one suspect out here, it could have gone totally different."

"Yes, sir. I understand."

Lee smiled at her. "I know you do," he said. "I tell you, at the halfway point of your training cycle, I'm already over the moon about your progress. You're going to make an excellent agent. Good work."

"Thank you, sir," she said.

Lee took his leave and walked elsewhere into the building, speaking with another instructor. As they started to file out, Harry came over to her, still grimacing a bit.

"Well done," he said. "It doesn't hurt half as bad when the person that came out on top is exceptionally pretty."

She rolled her eyes at him and holstered her Glock. "Flattery is useless," she said. "Flattery, as they say, gets you nowhere."

"I know," Harry said. "But would it at least get me a drink?"

She grinned. "If you're paying."

"Yeah, I'll pay," he agreed. "I wouldn't want you to kick my ass."

They exited the building and walked back out into the rain. Now that the drill was over, the rain was almost refreshing. And with several instructors and consultant agents skimming the grounds to end the night, she finally allowed herself to feel proud of herself.

Eleven weeks in, she had passed through the majority of the classroom-oriented part of her Academy training. She was almost there…about nine weeks away from wrapping up the course and potentially becoming a field agent for the FBI.

She suddenly wondered why she'd waited so long to leave Nebraska. When Ellington had recommended her for the Academy, it had essentially been her golden ticket, the push she needed to test herself, to break out of what had been comfortable and safe. She'd gotten rid of the job, the boyfriend, the apartment…and she'd picked up a new life.

She thought of the flat expanse of land, the cornfields, and the open blue skies that she had left behind. While they held their own specific beauty, it had, in a way, been a prison for her.

It was all behind her now.

Now that she was free, there was nothing left to hold her back.

*

The rest of her day proceeded with physical training: push-ups, sprints, crunches, more sprints, and selective weights. For her first few days at the Academy, she had hated this sort of training. But as her body and mind had gotten used to it, it seemed to her that she actually *craved* it.

Everything was done with speed and precision. She ran through fifty push-ups so fast that she wasn't aware of the burning in her upper arms until she was done with them and headed for the mud-flecked obstacle course. With just about any sort of physical activity, she had gotten into the mindset of thinking that she wasn't really pushing herself until her arms and legs were trembling and her abs felt like slabs of serrated meat.

There were sixty trainees in her unit and she was one of only nine women. This did not bother her, probably because her time in Nebraska had hardened her to not really caring about the gender of the people she worked with. She simply kept her head down and worked to the best of her abilities, which, she wasn't too proud to say, was pretty exceptional.

When the instructor called time on her last circuit—a two-mile run through muddy trails and forest—the class broke apart and went their separate ways. Mackenzie, on the other hand, took a seat on one of the benches along the edge of the course and stretched her legs out. With nothing much else going on for the day and still pumped from her successful stint in Hogan's Alley, she figured she'd head out for one last run.

As much as she hated to admit it, she had become one of those people that liked to run. While she wouldn't be enlisting in any themed marathons anytime soon, she had come to appreciate the act. Outside of the required laps and courses in her training, she found time to run along the wooded trails of the campus that sat six miles away from the FBI headquarters and, subsequently, about eight miles away from her new Quantico apartment.

With her workout tank top drenched in sweat and a flush in her face, she rounded out her day with a final sprint around the obstacle course, leaving the hills, fallen logs, and nets out of it. As she did, she noticed two different men watching her—not out of some sort of lustful daydreams, but in a sort of awe that, quite frankly, spurred her on.

Although, truth be told, she wouldn't mind a few lustful glances here and there. This new svelte body she had worked so hard for deserved to be appreciated. It was weird to feel so comfortable in her own skin, but she was growing to like it. She knew Harry Dougan liked it, too. But so far, he'd said nothing. Even if he *were* to say something, Mackenzie wasn't sure what she would say in return.

When her last run (just under two miles) was wrapped up, she showered in the training facilities and grabbed a pack of crackers from the vending machine on her way out. She had the rest of the day at her disposal; four hours to do whatever she wanted before hitting the treadmill at the gym—a little routine she'd managed to fall into just to stay one step ahead of everyone else.

What to do with the rest of her day? Maybe she could finally finish unpacking. There were still six boxes in her apartment that she had not cracked the packing tape to. That would be the smart thing to do. But she also wondered what Harry was up to this evening, if he would hold good for his drinks request. Did he mean tonight or some other night?

And, beyond that, she wondered what Agent Ellington was doing.

She and Ellington had nearly met up a few times but it had never stuck—likely for the best, as far as Mackenzie was concerned. She could go the rest of her life without being reminded of the embarrassment that had occurred between them back in Nebraska.

As she tried to decide what to do with her afternoon, she headed for her car. As she slid the key into the door lock, she saw a familiar face go jogging by. The jogger, a fellow agent-in-training named Colby Stinson, saw her looking and smiled. She jogged over to Mackenzie's car with energy that made Mackenzie think that Colby was starting her run, not wrapping it up.

"Hey there," Colby said. "Did the class leave you behind?"

"No. I snuck in an extra run."

"Well, of course you did."

"What's that supposed to mean?" Mackenzie asked. She and Colby knew one another fairly well, although it might be a long shot to say that they were *friends*. She was never sure when Colby was being funny or trying to get a rise out of her.

"It means that you're super-driven and a bit of an overachiever," Colby said.

"Guilty."

"So what are you doing?" Colby asked. She then pointed to the pack of crackers in Mackenzie's hand. "Is that lunch?"

"It is," she said. "Sad, huh?"

"A bit. Why don't we go grab something? Pizza sounds awesome to me."

Pizza sounded good to Mackenzie, too. But she really didn't feel like suffering through small talk, especially not with a woman that tended to lean a little too close to the gossipy side of conversation. Yet, on the other hand, she also knew that she needed more in her life than training, extra training, and holing herself up in her apartment.

"Yeah, let's do that," Mackenzie said.

It was a small victory—stepping out of her comfort zone and trying to make friends in this new place, in this new chapter of her life. But with each step, a new page was turned and she was, quite frankly, eager to start writing.

*

Donnie's Pizza Place was only half full when Mackenzie and Colby arrived there in the afternoon, the lunch crowd thinning out. They grabbed a table in the back and ordered a pizza. Mackenzie allowed herself to relax, resting her sore legs and arms, but was not able to enjoy it for long.

Colby sat forward and sighed. "So, can we address the elephant in the room?"

"There's an elephant?" Mackenzie asked.

"There is," Colby said. "But it's dressed in all black and sort of blends in most of the time."

"Okay," Mackenzie said. "Explain this elephant to me. And tell me why you're waiting until now to mention it."

"Something I never told you is that the first day you showed up at the Academy, I knew who you were. Just about everybody did. There was a lot of whispering. And that's why I'm waiting to tell you now. As we get to the end of this, I don't know how it is going to affect things."

"What whispering?" Mackenzie asked, pretty sure she already knew where this was going.

"Well, the important parts are about the Scarecrow Killer and the meek little lady that bagged him. A little lady that was so good being a detective in Nebraska that the FBI came calling."

"That's a rather glorified version of it, but yes…I recognize that elephant. You said *the important parts*, though. Are there other parts?"

Colby looked suddenly uncomfortable. She tucked a strand of her brown hair nervously behind her ear. "Well, there are rumors. I've heard some agent played a hand in getting you on board. And…well, we're in a male-driven environment. You can imagine how the rumors go."

Mackenzie rolled her eyes, finding herself embarrassed. She had never stopped to wonder what sorts of hushed rumors might have been circulating about her and Ellington, the agent that had indeed played a large part in getting her a shot at the Bureau.

"Sorry," Colby said. "Should I not have said anything?"

Mackenzie shrugged. "It's okay. I guess we all have our stories."

Apparently sensing that she may have said too much, Colby looked at the table and sipped nervously from her soda. "Sorry," she said softly. "I just thought you should know. You're the first real friend I've made here and I wanted to be as blunt as possible."

"Ditto," Mackenzie said.

"We good?" Colby asked.

"Yeah. Now how about you throw out some other topic to talk about?"

"Oh, that's easy," Colby said. "Tell me about you and Harry."

"Harry Dougan?" Mackenzie asked.

"Yes. The would-be agent that seems to undress you with his eyes every time you're in the same room together."

"Nothing to tell," Mackenzie said.

Colby smiled and rolled her eyes. "If you say so."

"No, really. He's not my type."

"Maybe you're not *his* type," Colby pointed out. "Maybe he just wants to see you naked. I wonder…what type *are* you? Deep and psychological, I bet."

"Why do you say that?" Mackenzie asked.

"Because of your interests and tendency to excel in profiling courses and scenarios."

"I think that's a common misconception about anyone interested in profiling," Mackenzie said. "If you need proof, I can point you to at least three aging men on the Nebraska State Police."

Conversation dwindled down to the mundane after that—their classes, their instructors, and so forth. But all the while, Mackenzie seethed on the inside. The rumors Colby had mentioned were the exact reason she had decided to stay under everyone's radar. She

13

had not gone out of her way to make many friends—a decision that *should* have afforded her plenty of time to get her apartment set up.

And under it all was Ellington...the man that had come into Nebraska and changed her world. It sounded clichéd to think such a thing, but it's essentially what happened. And the fact that she still couldn't get him out of her head was slightly nauseating.

Even as she and Colby shared pleasantries as they finished their lunch, Mackenzie wondered what Ellington was up to. She also wondered what *she* would be doing right now if he had not come strolling through Nebraska during her attempt to bring down the Scarecrow Killer. It was not a pleasant image: she'd probably still be driving those agonizingly straight roads, bordered by either sky, fields, or corn. And she'd likely be partnered with some chauvinist prick that was just a younger and more stubborn version of Porter, her old partner.

She did not miss Nebraska. She did not miss the routines of the job she'd had there, and she certainly did not miss the mindset. What she *did* miss, though, was knowing that she fit in. More than that, she was in the top tier of people in her department. Here in Quantico, that wasn't true. Here, she had massive competition and she had to fight to stay at the top.

Fortunately, she was more than up for the challenge and was happily leaving the Scarecrow Killer and her life before his arrest behind.

Now, if she could only get the nightmares to stop.

CHAPTER TWO

The next morning started bright and early with weapons training, something Mackenzie was finding that she was quite adept at. She'd always been a decent shot, but with the proper instruction and a class of twenty-two other hopefuls competing with her, she got eerily good. She still favored the Sig Sauer that she'd used in Nebraska and had been pleased to find that the Bureau's standard-issue sidearm was a Glock—not too dissimilar.

She stared down the paper target at the end of the firing corridor. A long sheet of paper hung stationary from the mechanized rack twenty yards away. She took aim, fired three times in rapid succession, and then put her gun down. The thrum of the shots rang out in her hands, a sensation she had come to enjoy.

When the green light at the back of the corridor gave her the go-ahead, she pushed a button on the small panel in front of her and brought the target up. It scaled forward and as it got closer, she could see where three holes had appeared in the paper target. It was the representation of a man's figure from the waist up. Two shots had landed high in the chest while the other had grazed the left shoulder. These were okay shots (not great) and while she was a little disappointed with the stray chest shots, she knew that she was doing much better than she had during her first shooting range session.

Eleven weeks. She'd been here for eleven weeks and was still learning. She was upset with the stray chest shots because those could be fatal. She had been trained to shoot to only take a suspect down—to deliver the fatal shot to the chest or head under the direst of circumstances.

Her instinct was getting better. She smiled at the paper target and then looked at the small control box in front of her where a box of ammunition waited. She reloaded the Glock and then pressed a button to send out another target. She let this one go back twenty-five yards.

She waited for the red light on the panel to turn to green and then turned her back. She took a breath, wheeled around, and fired off three more shots.

A neat row of bullet holes formed just below the figure's shoulder.

Much better, Mackenzie thought.

Satisfied, she removed her ear and eye protectors. She then tidied up her station and pressed another button on the control panel that brought the target forward on the motorized pulley system that carried out the targets. She took the target down, folded it, and placed it in the small book bag she carried just about everywhere.

She'd been coming to the range during her free time to sharpen skills that she felt she was a bit behind on when it came to the others in her class. She was one of the oldest there and rumors had circled through the grapevine already—rumors about how she had been headhunted from a miserable little PD in Nebraska right after wrapping up the Scarecrow Killer case. She was somewhere in the middle of the class average as far as firearms skill and was determined to be among the best by the time her Academy training came to an end.

She had to prove herself. And that was fine with her.

*

After the shooting range, Mackenzie wasted no time in heading to her final class-based course, a session on psychology that was taught by Samuel McClarren. McClarren was a sixty-six-year-old former agent and best-selling author, having penned six *New York Times* bestsellers about the psychological makeup of some of the most vicious serial killers of the past one hundred years. Mackenzie had read everything the man had written and could listen to him lecture for hours on end. It was by far her favorite course and although the assistant director had felt she didn't need the course based on her resume and work history, she had jumped at the chance to take it.

As usual, she was among the first in class, sitting near the front. She readied her notebook and pen while a few others trickled in and set up their MacBooks. As she waited, Samuel McClarren took to his podium. Behind Mackenzie, the class of forty-two students waited with anticipation; every single one of them seemed to hang on his every word when he spoke.

"We wrapped up the psychological constructs that we believe were driving Ed Gein yesterday, much to the delight of some of you with weaker stomachs," McClarren said. "And today, it's not going to get much better, as we dip into the often underrated yet incredibly twisted mind of John Wayne Gacy. Twenty-six recorded victims, killed by either strangulation or asphyxiation by use of a tourniquet. From the boards beneath his house to the Des Plaines River, he scattered his victims in various spots after they were killed. And, of course, there's what most people think of when they hear his name—the clown makeup. At its root, the Gacy case is a clinic on psychological breaks."

And so the class went, McClarren speaking while students feverishly took notes. As usual, the hour and fifteen minutes sped by and Mackenzie found herself wanting to hear more. On a few occasions, McClarren's class had brought up memories of her hunt for the Scarecrow Killer, particularly when she had revisited the murder sites in an attempt to get inside the mind of a killer. She had always known she'd had a knack for this sort of thing but had tried to keep it quiet. It scared her from time to time and was a bit morbid, so she kept it close to her chest.

When the session was over, Mackenzie packed up her things and headed for the door. She was still processing the lecture as she passed through into the hallway and didn't see the man standing by the edge of the doorway. In fact, she didn't notice him until he called out her name.

"Mackenzie! Hey, wait up."

She stopped at the sound of her name, turning around and spotting a familiar face in the small crowd.

Agent Ellington was following behind her. Seeing him was such a surprise that she literally stood motionless for a moment, trying to figure out why he was here. As she remained frozen, he gave her a timid smile and approached her quickly. Another man was with him, trailing behind.

"Agent Ellington," Mackenzie said. "How are you?"

"I'm good," he said. "Yourself?"

"Pretty good. What are you doing here? A refresher course?" she asked, trying to inject some humor.

"No, not so much," Ellington said. He gave her another smile and it reminded her all over again why she had taken the chance and made a fool of herself with him three months ago. He gestured to the man beside him and said, "Mackenzie White, I'd like you to meet Special Agent Bryers."

Bryers stepped forward and extended his hand. Mackenzie shook it as she took a moment to study the man. He looked to be in his early fifties. He had a mostly gray moustache and friendly blue eyes. She could tell right away that he was likely mild-mannered and one of the true southern gentlemen she had heard so much about since moving to Virginia.

"Pleased to meet you," Bryers said as they shook.

With that introduction out of the way, Ellington was back to business as usual. "Are you busy right now?" he asked Mackenzie.

"Not at the moment," she answered.

"Well, if you have a minute, Agent Bryers and I would like to speak with you about something."

Mackenzie saw the flash of doubt in Bryers's face as Ellington said this. Come to think of it, Bryers looked a little uncomfortable. Maybe *that* was why he seemed so timid.

"Sure," she said.

"Come on," Ellington said, waving her toward the small study area near the back of the building. "I'll buy you a coffee."

Mackenzie remembered the last time Ellington had showed such an interest in her; it had gotten her here, to nearly having her dream of being an FBI agent and living in the ebb and flow of it all. So to follow him now only made sense. She did so, casting a glance at Agent Bryers as they went and wondering why he looked so uneasy.

*

"So, you're pretty close, aren't you?" Ellington asked as the three of them sat down with their cups of coffee that Ellington had purchased from the tiny coffee bar.

"Eight weeks left," she said.

"Counter-terrorism, fifteen simulation hours, and about twelve shooting range hours left, right?" Ellington asked.

"And you know this how?" Mackenzie asked, concerned.

Ellington shrugged and gave a smirk. "I've made it my hobby to sort of keep tabs on you since you arrived here. I recommended you, so my ass is sort of on the line. You're impressing just about everyone that matters. Everything is really just a formality at this point. Unless you manage to crash and burn these last eight weeks, I'd say you're as good as in."

He took a deep breath and seemed to brace himself.

"Which brings us around to why I wanted to speak with you. Agent Bryers here is in a bit of a predicament and might need your help. But I'll let him explain that to you."

Bryers still looked unsure of the situation. It even showed as he set his coffee cup down and took a few seconds to start speaking.

"Well, as Agent Ellington says, you *have* been impressing the people that matter. In the last two days, I've had your name come up three times."

"In what regard?" she asked, a bit nervous.

"I'm on a case right now that has my partner of thirteen years turning away from the Bureau," Bryers explained. "He's close to retirement age anyway, so it's not much of a surprise. I love the guy like a brother, but he's had enough. He's seen enough during his twenty-eight years as an agent and did not want one more nightmare following him into retirement. So that, of course, leaves the gap open for a partner to step in and fill his shoes. It would not be a permanent partnership—just long enough to hopefully wrap up this current case."

Mackenzie felt a flutter of excitement in her heart and knew that she had to keep it in check before her need to please and impress took over. "That's why my name has come up?" she asked.

"That's right," Bryers said.

"But there have to be several experienced agents that could fill the role better than me."

"There probably *are* more appropriate agents," Ellington said matter-of-factly. "But so far as we can tell, this case mirrors the Scarecrow Killer case in more than a few ways. That, plus the fact that your name is getting around, has a lot of higher-ups thinking that you'd be a perfect fit."

"But I'm not an agent yet," Mackenzie pointed out. "I mean, with something like this, can you really afford to wait eight weeks?"

"We wouldn't be waiting," Ellington said. "And at the risk of sounding pompous, this isn't an offer the Bureau would hand out to just anyone. An opportunity like this—well, I'd bet anyone in that class you just stepped out of would kill to have it. It's incredibly unorthodox and a few important people are sort of looking the other way."

"It just seems…unethical," Mackenzie said.

"It is," Ellington said. "It's *technically* illegal in a few ways. But we can't look past the similarities between this case and what you wrapped up in Nebraska. It's either slip you in under the radar right now or wait about three or four days and hope to line Agent Bryers up with a new partner. And time is of the essence."

Of course she wanted the opportunity, but it felt too fast. It felt rushed.

"Do I have time to think it over?" she asked.

"No," Ellington said. "In fact, after this meeting, I'm having the case files delivered to your apartment to go over. I'll give you a few hours to look them over and then contact you at the end of the day for an answer. But, Mackenzie…I'd strongly suggest you take this."

She knew she would, but didn't want to seem too anxious or cocky. Plus, there *was* a degree of nervousness that was starting to set in. This was the big-time. And for an agent as seasoned as Bryers to want her help...well, that was simply amazing.

"Here's the gist," Bryers said, leaning in across the table and lowering his voice. "So far, we have two bodies that have shown up in the same landfill. Both have been young women—one was twenty-two, the other nineteen. They were found naked and with bruises all over them. The most recent showed signs of molestation but no trace of bodily fluids. The bodies appeared about two and a half months apart, but the fact that they showed up in the same dump with the same sort of bruising..."

"Not a coincidence," Mackenzie said, thinking it over.

"No, probably not," Bryers said. "So tell me...let's say this was your case. It *just* got handed to you. What's the first thing you'd do?"

It took her less than three seconds to come up with an answer. When she gave it, she felt herself slip into a sort of zone—a sense that she *knew* she was right. If there had been any doubt that she was going to accept this opportunity, it was erased as she gave her answer.

"I'd start at the landfill," she said. "I'd want to see the area for myself, through my own eyes. I'd then want to speak with family members. Were either of the women married?"

"The twenty-two-year-old," Ellington said. "She'd been married for sixteen months."

"Then yes," Mackenzie said. "I'd start at the landfill and then speak to the husband."

Ellington and Bryers gave one another a knowing look. Ellington nodded and drummed his hands on the table. "You in?" he asked.

"I'm in," she said, unable to keep her excitement at bay much longer.

"Good," Bryers said. He reached into his pocket and slid a set of keys across the table. "No sense in wasting time. Let's get going."

CHAPTER THREE

It was 1:35 when they reached the landfill. The eighty-five-degree weather enhanced the stink of the place, and the flies were so loud it was like some bizarre music. Mackenzie had driven while Bryers sat in the passenger seat, filling her in on the details of the case.

By the time they stepped out of the car and approached the dumps, Mackenzie thought she had Bryers pegged. He was, for the most part, a by-the-books sort of man. He would not come out and say as much, but he was extremely nervous about having her ride along with him, even if those in the know had approved it with blind eyes. It was evident in his posture and the fleeting glances he gave her.

Mackenzie walked slowly while Bryers approached the large green bins. He walked toward them as if he worked there. She had to remind herself that he'd been to the scene once before. He knew what to expect, making her feel very much like a novice—which she was, actually.

She took a moment to really study the place, having never taken the time to study landfills before. The area she and Bryers currently stood in—the portion of the landfill that allowed traffic—was really nothing more than a dump. Six economy-sized metal dumpsters lined the place, all set within a hollow space within the grounds. Behind the dumps, she could see the area below where state trucks came to pick up the haul. To allow for these hollow areas that hid most of the dumpsters, the paved entryway and lot took on the shape of a well-maintained hill; the area she and Bryers currently stood on was the summit while the road through the landfill led further back, wound around, and spit cars out behind the dumpsters into a road that led back out to the highway.

Mackenzie scanned the ground. Where she stood was nothing more than packed dirt that gave way to gravel and then tar around the other side of the bins. She was standing on the dirt portion and looking down to the tire tracks that were embedded like ghost prints along the ground. The criss-crossing and jumbled passage of countless tire tracks was going to make it very hard to identify a reliable print. It had been dry and hot lately; the last rainfall had been about a week ago and that had only been a drizzle. Dry ground was going to make this significantly harder.

Feeling that getting suitable prints out of the mess was going to be next to impossible, she joined Bryers by the dump he was standing by.

"The body was found in this one," Bryers said. "Forensics already lifted the blood samples and took the prints. The victim's name was Susan Kellerman, twenty-two years old, a resident of Georgetown."

Mackenzie nodded, still saying nothing. She shifted her priorities as she looked into the dump. She was working with people from the FBI now so she felt comfortable skipping ahead a few steps. She wouldn't waste her time looking for the obvious. Those that had come before her—probably including Bryers—had already done the legwork. Therefore, Mackenzie tried to focus on the obscure...on the things that might have been overlooked.

After about a minute of looking around the immediate area, Mackenzie thought she knew everything there was to know. And so far, it wasn't much.

"So tell me," Bryers said. "If you had to guess, what's the significance of the killer dumping his bodies here?"

"I don't think it's a matter of convenience," Mackenzie said. "I think he's trying to play it safe. He's discarding the bodies here because he wants to get rid of them. I'd also guess he lives nearby...no more than twenty or thirty miles. I don't think he'd drive that far off just to dispose of a body...especially at night."

"Why at night?" Bryers asked.

Mackenzie knew that he was testing her and didn't mind. Given the amazing opportunity she had been handed, she expected some ribbing.

"Because he'd almost *have* to come during the night to dump a body. Doing it in the light of day while there are workers here would be stupid."

"So you think he's smart?"

"Not necessarily. He's cautious and careful. And that's not the same as *smart*."

"I saw you scouring for tracks," he said. "We tried and there was nothing. There are just too many."

"Yeah, it would be difficult," she said. "Of course, like I said, I'd assume the body was dumped after hours. Is that the assumption you're going on?"

"It is."

"So there would be no prints here," Mackenzie pointed out.

He smiled at her. "That's right," he said. "No tire tracks anyway. But *foot*prints would. Not that it matters. There are too many of those, too."

Mackenzie nodded, feeling stupid for having missed such an obvious fact. But right away, that sent her mind down a different path.

"Well, it's not like he carried the body over his shoulders," Mackenzie said. "His tire tracks *would* be somewhere. Not here, but maybe just outside of the gate. We could then try to compare and contrast between tracks we find stopped outside the gate and tracks here in this dirt. We could even look right around the edge of the fence for any indication of impact from where he almost certainly threw or dropped the body over."

"That's good thinking," Bryers said, clearly amused. "That's a detail the guys from the print lab got, but I managed to overlook. But yes, you're right. He would have had to stop his car outside of the gate. So the thinking is that if we find tracks that come to the gate, stop, then turn around, that could be our guy."

"*Could* be," Mackenzie said.

"So you're thinking along the right lines, but there's nothing new. What else you got?"

He wasn't being rude or dismissive; she knew this from his tone alone. He was simply trying to urge her on, to motivate her to keep going.

"Do we know how many vehicles come through here on any given day?"

"Approximately eleven hundred or so," Bryers said. "Still, if we can get prints that come close to the gate and then just *stop…*"

"It could be a start."

"That's the hope," Bryers said. "We've had a team working on that since yesterday afternoon and we still don't have any leads."

"I can take a look if you'd like," Mackenzie said.

"Knock yourself out," Bryers said. "But you're working with the Bureau now, Ms. White. Don't overwork yourself if there's another department that can handle it better than you can."

Mackenzie looked back into the dumpster, trying to make sense of the crushed shapes of trash inside. A young woman had been there recently, her body nude and slightly beaten. She'd been discarded in the same place people dumped their refuse, the things they no longer needed. Maybe the killer was trying to speculate that the women he had killed were no better than common household trash.

She almost wished she had been here when Bryers and his soon-to-be-retired friend had come out. Maybe then she'd have more to go on. Maybe then she could help lead Bryers closer to a suspect. But for now, at least she had proven herself rather quickly with her perceptions regarding the tire tracks.

She turned back around to him and saw that he was standing idly, peering back toward the gate. It was clear that he was giving her some time to process. She appreciated it, but again, it made her very aware just how much of a rookie she was.

She ventured down to the chain-link fence that surrounded the dump. She started at the gate where vehicles came through and worked her way to the left. She looked around the bottom edge of the fence for a few seconds before another thought hit her.

He'd have to climb the fence, she thought.

She then started investigating the fence. She wasn't sure what she was looking for. Maybe stray dirt or fibers on the chain links. Anything she found would be a long shot, but it would be something.

It took less than two minutes before she came across something of interest. It was so infinitesimal that she almost ignored it completely. But as she stepped closer, she saw that it might be more helpful than she had originally thought.

About five feet off the ground and six feet to the left of the entry gate, a single strand of white fabric clung to one of the diamond shapes in the fence. The fabric itself might not yield any results but this at least gave them a great place to start dusting for fingerprints.

"Agent Bryers?" she said.

He came over slowly, as if he wasn't expecting much. As he got closer, she heard him make a *hmmm* sound as he looked at the piece of fabric.

"Great work, Ms. White," he said.

"Please, just Mackenzie," she said. "Mac, if you're feeling adventurous."

"What do you think it is?" he asked.

"Maybe nothing. Buy maybe a strand of clothing from someone that recently scaled the fence. The fabric may be useless, but it gives us a concentrated area to focus on for fingerprints."

"There's a small evidence kit in the trunk of the car. Can you retrieve it while I call this in?"

"Sure," she said, heading back to the car.

By the time she returned to him, he was already ending the call. Everything with Bryers seemed to be quick and efficient. It was one of the things she was quickly starting to like about him.

"Okay, Mac," he said. "Now let's continue down the trail you spelled out earlier today. The victim's husband lives about twenty minutes away from here. You up for it?"

"I am," Mackenzie said.

They got back into the car and pulled out of the still-closed-down landfill. Overhead, a series of scavenger birds performed their duty diligently, watching the drama unfold below with uncaring eyes.

***

Caleb Kellerman already had visitors in the form of two policemen when Mackenzie and Bryers arrived at his home. He lived just outside of Georgetown in a two-story house that made for a cute starter home. Thinking that the Kellermans had only been married for a little over a year before his bride had been killed made Mackenzie feel sorry for the man, but also angry about what had happened.

A starter home that never got a chance to see what else it could be, Mackenzie thought as they stepped into the house. *How profoundly sad.*

They entered through the front door, stepping into a thin foyer that looked directly into the living room. Mackenzie could feel the creeping sense of loneliness and quiet that accompanied most residences shortly after a death. She hoped she'd eventually get used to it, but found it hard to believe.

Bryers made introductions with the police outside of the foyer and the boys in uniform seemed relieved to be asked to step aside. When they made their exit, Bryers and Mackenzie stepped into the living room. Mackenzie saw that Caleb Kellerman looked incredibly young; he could easily pass for eighteen with his clean-shaven look, Five Finger Death Punch T-shirt, and baggy camo shorts. Mackenzie was able to quickly look past his appearance, focusing instead on the indescribable grief she saw in the young man's face.

He looked up to them, waiting for either of them to speak. Mackenzie noticed Bryers giving her the go-ahead, nodding subtly in Caleb Kellerman's direction. She stepped forward, both terrified and flattered that she was being given such authority. Either Bryers thought a lot of her, or he was trying to make her uncomfortable.

25

"Mr. Kellerman, I'm Agent White, and this is Agent Bryers." She hesitated there for a moment. Had she really just called herself *Agent* White? It sort of had a nice ring to it. She skipped past this and continued on. "I know you're dealing with a loss that I won't even pretend to be able to understand," she said. She kept her tone soft, warm, but firm. "But if we want to find the person that did this, we really need to ask you some questions. Are you up for it?"

Caleb Kellerman nodded. "Anything I can do to make sure the man that did this is found," he said. "I'll do anything."

There was rage in his voice that made Mackenzie hope that someone would seek some sort of therapy for Caleb in the coming days. There was something in his eyes that looked nearly unhinged.

"Well, first of all, I need to know if Susan had any enemies…anyone that might be a rival of sorts."

"There were a few girls she went to high school with that would get pissy with her on Facebook," Caleb said. "It was usually over politics, though. And none of those girls would do it, anyway. It was just nasty arguments and things like that."

"And what about her job?" Mackenzie asked. "Did she enjoy it?"

Caleb shrugged. He sat back on the couch and tried to relax. His face, however, seemed resigned to a permanent frown. "She liked it about as much as any woman that went to college and lands a job that has nothing to do with her degree. It paid the bills and the bonuses were pretty good sometimes. The hours sucked, though."

"Did you know any of the people she worked with?" Mackenzie asked.

"No. I heard about them in the stories she'd bring home, but that was it."

Bryers chimed in next. His voice sounded very different in the still of the house as he used somber tones. "She was a saleswoman, correct? For A Better You University?"

"Yeah. I already gave the police her supervisor's number."

"We've had some people from the Bureau already speak with him," Bryers said.

"It won't matter," Caleb said. "No one at work killed her. I can guarantee it. I know it sounds stupid, but it's this feeling I have. Everyone at her work is nice…in the same boat we were in, trying to pay bills and make ends meet. Honest people, you know?"

For a moment, he teetered on the edge of weeping. He stifled it back, looked down to the floor to collect himself, and looked back up. The tears that he had barely suppressed floated along the edges of his eyes.

"Okay, then what can you think of that might lead us down the right path?" Bryers asked.

"I can't," Caleb said. "She had a sell sheet of the clients she was visiting that day, but no one can find it. The cops said it's probably because the killer took it and trashed it."

"That's probably the case," Mackenzie said.

"I still don't get it," Caleb said. "It still doesn't feel real. I'm waiting for her to come back through that door any minute now. The day she died…it started out just like any other day. She kissed me on the cheek as I was getting dressed for work and said goodbye. She left for the bus stop, and that was it. That was the last time I saw her."

Mackenzie saw that Caleb was on the verge of losing it and, as much as it seemed wrong to do so, she got in one last question before he collapsed.

"Bus stop?" she asked.

"Yeah, she rode the bus to the office every day; she caught the eight twenty to get to work on time. The car crapped out on us two months ago."

"Where's that bus stop located?" Bryers asked.

"Two blocks down," Caleb said. "It's one of those small vestibule-type deals." He then looked at Mackenzie and White, hope suddenly blooming in his eyes under the pain and hatred. "Why? Do you think it's important?"

"There's no way to know for sure," Mackenzie said. "But we'll keep you posted. Thank you for your time."

"Sure," Caleb said. "Hey…guys?"

"Yeah?" Mackenzie said.

"It's been more than three days now, right? Three days since I last saw her and almost two whole days since they found her body."

"That's right," Bryers said quietly.

"So is it too late? Is this bastard going to get away?"

"No," Mackenzie said. It was out of her mouth before she could stop it and she knew right away that she had made her first mistake in front of Bryers.

"We'll do the best we can," Bryers said, placing a gentle but urging hand on Mackenzie's shoulder. "Please call us if you think of anything that might help."

With that, they made their exit. Mackenzie shuddered a bit when she heard Caleb break down in a sobbing fit before they were able to shut the door behind them.

That sound did something to her…something that reminded her of home. The last time she'd felt such a thing was the moment back in Nebraska when she had become absolutely consumed with the task of stopping the Scarecrow Killer. She felt that all-consuming need again as they stepped out onto Caleb Kellerman's front steps, and she slowly realized that she would stop at nothing until she caught this killer.

CHAPTER FOUR

"You can't do that," Bryers said the moment they were back in the car, he taking the wheel.

"I can't do what?"

He sighed and tried his best to seem sincere rather than disciplinary. "I know you've probably never been in this exact situation before, but you can't tell the family of a victim that *no,* the killer isn't going to get away. You can't give them hope if there is none. Hell, even if there *is* hope, you can't say something like that."

"I know," she said, disappointed. "I knew it the moment the word was out of my mouth. I'm sorry."

"No need for apologies. Just try to keep your head on straight. Got it?"

"Got it."

Because Bryers knew the city better than Mackenzie, he drove them to the Department of Public Transportation. He drove with some urgency and requested that Mackenzie call ahead to make sure they could speak to someone that knew what they were talking about and could get them in and out of there in a hurry. It was such a simple method, but Mackenzie was impressed with the efficiency of it. It was a far cry from what she'd experienced in Nebraska for sure.

During the half hour drive, Bryers filled the car with conversation. He wanted to know all about her time on the force in Nebraska, most notably the Scarecrow Killer case. He asked about college and her interests. She was happy enough to give him the surface-level information but didn't go too deep—mainly because he wasn't going very deep himself.

In fact, Bryers seemed reserved. When Mackenzie asked him about his family, he kept it as general as he could without being rude. "A wife, two boys that are off to college, and a dog that's on its last legs."

Well, Mackenzie thought. *It's only our first day together and he doesn't know me at all—just what he read about me in the papers six months ago and from whatever is in my file with the Academy. I don't blame him for not opening up just yet.*

When they arrived at the Department of Public Transportation, Mackenzie still held a favorable opinion of the elder agent but there was a tension between them that she couldn't quite grasp. Maybe he didn't feel it; maybe it was just her. The fact that he had basically waved off any questions she asked him about his work made her

29

uncomfortable. It also made her quickly remember that this was not her job yet. She was simply riding along as a favor to Ellington, a way to test her wheels, so to speak.

She was also involved in all of this due to some shady dealings in back rooms where the higher-ups were taking a gamble on her. It added a whole new level of risk not only for her, but for the people she was working with—Bryers and Ellington included.

The Department of Transportation was located inside of a building with about ten other departments housed within it. Mackenzie followed Agent Bryers through the hallways as best she could. He walked quickly, nodding to people here and there as if he were familiar with the place. A few people seemed to recognize him, giving him quick smiles and waves here and there. The day was coming to an end, so people seemed to be milling about quickly, waiting for five o'clock.

As they came to the section of the building they needed, Mackenzie started to allow herself to appreciate the moment. Four hours ago, she'd been coming out of McClarren's class and now she was somehow knee deep in a homicide case, working with an agent that seemed to be well conditioned and damn good at his job.

They approached a counter where Bryers leaned slightly over it and eyed the young woman sitting behind a desk immediately in front of them. "We called about speaking to someone about the bus schedules," he explained to the woman. "Agents White and Bryers."

"Oh yes," the receptionist said. "You'll be speaking to Mrs. Percell. She is out back in the bus garage. It's all the way down the hall, down the stairs, and out the back."

They followed the receptionist's directions, heading to the back of the building where Mackenzie could already hear the humming of engines and the rumbling of machinery. The building was constructed in such a way that the noise was not at all noticeable in the busier, nicer parts of the building but here in the back, it sounded almost like an auto garage.

"When we meet this Mrs. Percell," Bryers said, "I want you to take the lead."

"Okay," Mackenzie said, still feeling like she was taking some sort of weird exam.

They took the stairs down, following a sign labeled *Garage / Bus Lot*. Downstairs, a thin hallway led into a small open office. A man in mechanic's scrubs stood behind an antiquated computer, typing something in. Through a large picture window, Mackenzie was able to look out into a large garage. Several city buses were parked there, undergoing maintenance. As she watched, a door in the back of the office opened and a cheerful-looking overweight woman entered from the garage.

"Are you the FBI folks?"

"That's us," Mackenzie said. Beside her, Bryers flashed his badge—probably because she didn't have one to show. Percell seemed satisfied with the credentials and started talking right away.

"I understand you have questions about the bus schedules and the rotation of drivers," she said.

"That's correct," Mackenzie replied. "We're hoping to find out what stop a certain bus made three mornings ago and, if possible, to get a word with the driver."

"Sure," she said. She went over to the small desk where the mechanic was typing and nudged him playfully. "Doug, let me take the wheel, would you?"

"Gladly," he said with a smile. He stepped away from the desk and headed out to the garage as Mrs. Percell sat down behind the computer. She hit a few keys and then looked up to them proudly, obviously glad to be of service.

"Where's the stop in question?"

"At the corner of Carlton and Queen Street," Mackenzie said.

"What time would the person have gotten on?"

"Eight twenty in the morning."

Mrs. Percell typed the information in quickly and scanned the screen for a moment before giving her answer. "That was bus number 2021, driven by Michael Garmond. That bus makes three stops before reporting back to that same bus stop for a nine thirty-five pickup."

"We need to speak with Mr. Garmond," Mackenzie said. "Could we have his information, please?"

"I can do better than that," Mrs. Percell said. "Michael is out in the garage right now, signing out for the day. Let me see if I can grab him for you."

"Thanks," Mackenzie said.

Mrs. Percell dashed to the garage door with speed that defied her size. Mackenzie and Bryers watched her amble expertly through the garage in search of Michael Garmond.

"If only everyone was that enthusiastic about helping the feds," Bryers said with a grin. "Trust me…don't get used to this."

In less than a minute, Mrs. Percell returned into the small office, followed by an elderly black man. He looked tired but, like Mrs. Percell, more than happy to help.

"Hey, folks," he said, giving a tired smile. "How can I help you?"

"We're looking for details about a woman that we are fairly confident got on your bus at the eight twenty stop at the corner of Carlton and Queen three mornings ago," Mackenzie said. "Do you think you could help us with that?"

"Probably," Michael said. "There aren't too many people at that stop in the mornings. I never get more than four or five."

Bryers pulled out his cell phone and thumbed through it for a bit, pulling up a photograph of Susan Kellerman. "This is her," he said. "Does she look familiar?"

"Hey, yeah, she does," Michael said, a bit too excited in Mackenzie's opinion. "Sweet girl. Always really nice."

"Do you recall where she got off the bus three mornings ago?"

"I do," Michael said. "And I thought it was weird because every other morning for about two weeks or so, she was getting off at another bus stop. I talked to her a bit one morning and found out she walked two blocks from her usual stop to work at some office. But three days ago, she got off at the station instead of a stop. I watched her hop on another bus. I kind of hoped she'd gotten some better job or something, so she was taking a different route."

"Where was that?" Mackenzie asked.

"Dupont Circle."

"What time would you say she got off the bus there?"

"Probably around eight forty-five or so," Michael answered. "No later than nine o'clock for sure."

"We can check that in our records," Mrs. Percell said.

"That would be great," Bryers said.

Mrs. Percell went back to work behind the grimy little desk as Michael looked at the agents forlornly. He looked back to the picture on Bryers's phone and frowned. "Something bad happened to her?" he asked.

"In fact, yes," Mackenzie said. "So if there's anything you can tell us about her that morning, that would be great."

"Well, she was carrying a case, like the kind salespeople carry around. Not like a briefcase, but a tacky case, you know? She sold stuff for a living—like health supplements and things like that. I was guessing she had a customer she was seeing."

"Do you know which bus she got on after yours?" Mackenzie asked.

"Well, I don't recall the number of the bus, but I remember seeing Black Mill Street up on the destination indicator in the windshield. I thought that was pretty sketchy…no reason for that pretty little thing to be going to that part of town."

"And why is that?"

"Well, the neighborhood itself is okay, I guess. The houses aren't too bad and I think most of the folks are decent people. But it's one of those places where the not-so nice people hang around and do their business. When I was trained for this job six years ago, they filled the drivers in on places to keep an eye out for danger. Black Mill Street was one of them."

Mackenzie thought all of this over and realized that they had gotten all of the valuable information there was to get from Michael Garmond. She wanted to seem efficient in front of Bryers but she also didn't want to seem as if she wasted time on trivial details.

"Thank you very much, Mr. Garmond," Mackenzie said.

From the desk, Mrs. Percell added: "The stop at Dupont Circle was at eight forty-eight, Agents."

When they turned and made their exit, they were quiet until they made it back to the stairs. When they started climbing them, it was Bryers who broke the silence.

"How long have you been in Quantico?" he asked.

"Eleven weeks."

"So you're probably not familiar with the outskirts of the city, huh?"

"No."

"Never been up to Black Mill Street?"

"Can't say that I have," Mackenzie said.

"You're not missing much. But hey, maybe we won't have to go that far. We'll start at Dupont Circle and have a look around. Maybe we can find something on the security cameras."

"Now?"

"Yes, now," Bryers said. There was an edge of annoyance to his voice, the first sign that he was beginning to tire of carting around the rookie no matter how promising she was. "When there's a killer on the loose, we don't really punch a clock."

Several retorts came to her tongue, but she kept them choked down. He was right, anyway. If she'd learned anything from her ordeal with the Scarecrow Killer, it was that when you were chasing down a killer that seemingly had no MO, every minute was precious.

CHAPTER FIVE

Dupont Circle Station was just starting to slow down from the busyness of the five o'clock afternoon rush when Mackenzie and Bryers arrived. The conversation along the way was once again surface-level and stale as Bryers remained quiet and reserved. As they stepped out of the car and walked toward the station, Mackenzie truly felt awkward for the first time. She didn't think he resented her yet, but he was likely having second thoughts about whatever scheme he and Ellington had cooked up.

Bryers finally cracked their silence as they entered the station. He stepped to the side of the doors and watched the crowd of people threading through the place.

"You familiar with this place?" he asked.

"No," Mackenzie said. "I've always gone through Union Station."

Bryers shrugged. "It doesn't matter which station you're at; there's always going to be a corner somewhere that's a little seedier than the rest of the place. The rough part is that it's usually well hidden."

"So you're thinking she was taken on her way back home? You think someone grabbed her here when she was in between buses?"

"It's a possibility. What do *you* think?"

"I think we should be checking Black Mill Street. You *and* the bus driver said the place was bad news."

"And we'll probably end up there," Bryers said. "But I'm playing a hunch here. You work this city long enough you start to accumulate a sort of hunch about certain things."

His cryptic talk was annoying, but she figured she could actually learn something if she could just shut up and watch. After a minute or so of standing by the doors and watching the crowd, Bryers moved slowly forward, motioning for Mackenzie to follow him. She stayed close, but not so close that she was crowding him. He walked through the crowd nonchalantly, as if he had no real purpose for being there. He blended in quite well; only someone who really took the time to study him might suspect that he was some sort of law enforcement official.

They made their way through the main concourse and out toward where six buses were waiting. Passengers were stepping off of two of the buses while the others idled, waiting for passengers. As they headed toward the buses, Mackenzie looked at the destination indicators above the windshields. As far as she could tell, the next stops for these buses were all within the DC historic district or Georgetown.

"Over here," Bryers said.

Mackenzie looked away from the buses and stayed behind Bryers as he walked further down the concourse. The buses were behind them now as the crowd thinned out a bit. Out of nowhere, the scene seemed to change simply by rounding a corner. There were fewer people in casual or business-casual attire. She saw a homeless man sitting against the wall and three teenagers dressed in mostly black, adorned with large earrings, nose piercings, and tattoos everywhere.

Bryers slowed as they rounded this corner, again taking in the scene. Mackenzie did the same, trying to observe the layout of the place and the makeup of the people the same way he did. It only took a few seconds before she saw something that instantly put her on guard.

A young man with a short, nearly military buzz haircut and dressed in a plain T-shirt and jeans was speaking to a girl that was surely no older than sixteen. Mackenzie knew the look on her face because it was easy to read on most girls her age: she was liking the attention the guy was giving her, but was also uncomfortable in being approached. She saw that the guy had a hand in his pocket. She was pretty sure he wasn't packing, but there were numerous other things that he could be concealing.

Without looking over his shoulder to speak to her, Bryers asked: "You see him?"

"Twenty-something buzz-cut speaking to the minor?" she said.

"Bingo."

Still, they did not move. Mackenzie knew why even though she already didn't like the way the scene was playing out. Bryers was waiting for the creep to make a move—to do something that would warrant someone of Bryers's authority to step in and intervene.

They watched the scene unfold as they did what they could to blend in. Mackenzie felt herself wanting to surge forward as it played out predictably. The guy inched closer and closer. He was doing a lot of smiling and trying to look the girl in the eyes. She smiled back flirtatiously but looked at the ground more than she looked at him.

Slowly, he reached out and touched her shoulder. His hand rested there for a while before the girl stepped awkwardly away. The creep followed up by laughing and then stepping into her, placing his arm around her. He tried pulling her close but the girl stepped away. A look of frustration flashed across the guy's face before he stepped forward again, with a bit of anger this time. When he reached out to put his arm around her again, Bryers stepped forward. Mackenzie followed along, trying to make herself remain in the role of a student.

"Is there a problem here?" Bryers asked, stepping into the girl's path. "Is this guy harassing you?"

The girl looked up, surprised. She looked instantly relieved but then looked back to the ground, maybe a little embarrassed.

"I don't think so," the girl said. "Some guys just don't take *no* for an answer."

"Shut up, bitch," the crewcut guy said. He then looked directly at Bryers and said: "What business is it of yours, anyway?"

Bryers withdrew his ID so fast that it was like watching a gunslinger go for his irons. "It's my business in more ways than you want to imagine," he said.

"Oh," crewcut said. "Well, I think I might—"

And then he turned and ran.

"Ah, hell," Bryers said. He started to take off after the young man but Mackenzie couldn't stay still any longer.

"You stay with the girl," she said. "I'll get him."

"Are you sure?" Bryers asked. "I don't know if—"

"I'm sure," she said, already starting to sprint after the suspect.

Without looking back for confirmation from Bryers, Mackenzie dashed forward. There wasn't much of a crowd assembled along the concourse, giving her few obstacles to contend with. Within two seconds, she knew she'd catch up to the creep easily. He was running on panic and fear while her own strides were balanced and controlled.

The idiot even stopped to look over his shoulder, further giving her the edge. When he saw that she was on his heels, he found another gear. But by then, Mackenzie already had him. She gave an extra push, finding her own next gear, and got within arms' reach of him. The few people standing in her way saw what was occurring and had stepped out of the way, mainly for their own safety but also to watch what might happen.

Her hand fell on his shoulder and all it took was a hard push downward to halt him. His feet slid out from underneath him and he went to the cement sidewalk on his back. He let out a cry that was nearly comical but the hard impactful noise of his body hitting the pavement was not funny at all.

She took a moment to gauge his condition and when she was confident he had broken nothing and was still coherent, she dropped a knee into his chest and looked back toward Bryers. He was jogging along, looking rather concerned. The girl they had perhaps rescued was striding along beside him. She looked a bit frightened but also excited. Mackenzie saw a bit of joy in her face when she spotted her would-be harasser pinned on the ground.

All around them, a few bystanders started to applaud. Others looked slightly horrified at what they had just witnessed. Bryers flashed his badge to the gathered crowd. "Get going," he said. "The show is over. Get moving, everyone."

When they started to break up and continue on their respective ways, Bryers came over to Mackenzie and dropped to a knee.

"Up, please," Bryers said curtly.

Mackenzie got up, trying to gauge the expression on his face. He was angry, that much was clear. She wondered if she had been a little too rough in bringing the suspect down. Or maybe she shouldn't have given chase without his express permission.

As she got to her feet, Bryers slowly helped the perp to his feet. Mackenzie saw that the guy was bleeding from a small cut along the right side of his head. That side of his face was also a little red. She was positive he'd have one hell of a bruise there tomorrow.

"Come with me for a second," Bryers said.

"Get your hands off of me, man!"

Bryers grabbed the guy's arm and drew him close. "Remember that badge I showed you? The one that sent you running like a lunatic? That badge says you listen to me or find yourself in a world of trouble. Got me?"

"Whatever, man," the guy said. He stopped struggling against Bryers then and allowed himself to be led away from the gathering crowd.

Bryers cut his eyes in Mackenzie's direction but didn't *actually* look at her. It was pretty clear that he was pissed. "Check out the girl while I handle this mess," he said.

It was not a question, not a request...it was a demand. He was asking her to babysit while he questioned the suspect. And maybe she deserved it...but it felt awful.

Mackenzie watched him go as she walked over to the girl. She tried to ignore Bryers's reaction as she led the girl to a nearby bench. They sat down together but it was clear that the girl wanted to be long gone.

"Are you okay?" Mackenzie asked.

"I'm fine," she said.

"Do you know that guy?" Mackenzie asked.

"No. He just came up to me when I got off of the bus and started talking to me."

"What did he talk about?"

"Oh, he didn't waste any time. He said how pretty I was and then asked how old I was. When I told him I was sixteen, he asked if I was looking to make some easy money."

"Do you have a parent around here anywhere?"

"Not here, no. I'm visiting my dad. Mom tossed me on a bus to visit him for the weekend. But dear old Dad is working late. So I was going to have to catch a cab from here."

"What's your name?" Mackenzie asked.

The girl looked suspiciously at her but gave her name anyway...or what she wanted them to think her name was. "Jen," she said.

"Well, how about we call you that cab, Jen?" Mackenzie asked.

Jen looked at her like she was stupid. "That would be great. Thanks."

Mackenzie pulled out her phone and started to dial when Jen stopped her.

"That guy...do you think he would have hurt me if you guys hadn't showed up?"

"There's no way to know for sure," Mackenzie said.

"Well, thanks."

Mackenzie nodded and placed the call to the cab company. When the phone started ringing in her ear, she looked back over to Bryers. She saw that he'd placed the suspect in handcuffs and had him pressed against the wall. Bryers, meanwhile, was on his phone to call it in.

And maybe, Mackenzie thought, *to complain about my carelessness with a suspect.*

And just like that, Mackenzie started to feel this amazing opportunity she had been handed slipping right out of her hands.

CHAPTER SIX

When Mackenzie finally arrived at her apartment, she closed the door behind her and simply stood there for a moment. The final eight hours of her day had been surreal—like some of the dreams she'd had in high school of becoming an FBI agent had finally been granted and she wasn't sure how to handle it. More than that, she also felt the threat of it all being torn out from under her because of a split second's poor judgment.

And behind it all was the case. Whether she remained on it or not remained to be seen, but there was still someone out there that had killed two women and tossed them aside in public landfills. If she was taken off of the case after getting a peek into the case without the chance to properly solve it, she wasn't sure how she'd react.

With a shuddering sigh, she stepped into the apartment. She looked at the few boxes of things she had not yet unpacked—they were pushed into the far corner of the living room where she guessed she'd one day put a TV—assuming she stayed in Quantico after the tumultuous afternoon she'd had. She had planned on unpacking those three boxes tonight but was too tired...yet, at the same time, far too exhilarated to even think about unpacking boxes of belongings containing items from what she was already thinking of as *her old life.*

With her wits once again regained, she placed the folder Bryers had given her on the coffee table in front of the couch. It was still littered with a few things that had been unpacked but not yet put away. She figured there was no sense in *assuming* she'd be yanked from the case. It was better to be proactive rather than brooding and defeated.

Besides...Bryers had been his usual quiet self on the way back from the station. The suspect had been taken into custody and that was all that she knew. If any information had come forth about the suspect, his history, or what he had planned to do with sixteen-year-old Jen, no one had bothered to inform her.

Mackenzie started looking through the scant information on the body of Susan Kellerman and the other body that had been discovered three months before, a nineteen-year-old named Shanda Elliot.

But she couldn't even keep her mind focused enough for that. She would look at the facts in front of her and then try to make sense of how her life had drastically changed in the last half a day or so. She toyed with putting on some coffee, but it was nearly nine o'clock by that point and she wanted to make sure she was good and rested for tomorrow.

Bryers had asked her to meet him in the reception area at the FBI Building, which was, in and of itself, a pretty big deal. The fact that he wanted to meet her at eight o'clock to start the day as soon as possible meant something else though…what, she wasn't sure. But she got the feeling that if today was a test of sorts, tomorrow would yield that test's results.

With one final scan of the material in the folder, she decided to call it a night. She closed the folder, set it to the side (away from the scattered detritus of her former life), and stood up from the couch. As she made her way to the small bedroom she had learned to call home over the last several months, her cell phone started ringing. It was in her hand when it rang and the suddenness of it made her jump, proving that she did indeed need to catch up on her sleep.

She looked at the display and saw that it was Zack calling. It was funny, but it actually took her about two seconds to make a connection—and it made her feel wonderful.

Zack? Who is Z—oh yeah, him…

They'd spoken only twice since she moved: once during her very brief time in Dallas and once about three months ago. Both conversations had been depressing and filled with accusations and pity from Zack's end. He had moaned about their need to move on while also talking about how she had been a coward for running away like she had. He hadn't said as much, but she had deciphered the true meaning behind it all; she had wounded his stupid male pride because how dare a woman so badly alter the course of his lazy and lackluster life? He was heartbroken and had no idea how to handle it because he'd never made himself open and vulnerable.

She ignored the call and breathed a sigh of relief when she did not hear the *beep* to let her know that she had a new voicemail.

She went into the bedroom, headed into the even smaller bathroom, and got ready for bed. As she settled under the sheets moments later, she thought of Zack for a moment and how easy it was to escape the ghosts of your past so long as you were able to control the frequency of their haunting.

Of course, she also knew that there were sometimes ghosts that hung on forever, until they felt like someone latched to your back, dragging you down and reminding you that they'd be there forever and there was no hope for escape.

***

Mackenzie walked into her parents' bedroom. The smell of blood clung to the air and her nine-year-old self already knew the smell for what it was before she saw it all over the bed sheets and walls. She saw her father on the bed and her dream-self didn't even flinch. She stepped to the side of the bed, barely giving her father a glance; in dreams she'd had before she always looked at him and she knew it would be the same now. Dead eyes and an almost unbelievably black hole in the top of his head. The gun he supposedly used to do it to himself was somewhere on the bed, hidden among the twisted sheets like a coiled snake, watching.

Mackenzie walked past her dead father and to the window that sat just slightly to the left of the bed. She pulled the drawn curtain aside and looked out. She could see something in the front yard, some shape shrouded by shadows. A car approached from the driveway, splashing headlights across the figure. It was a woman, tied to a post, stripped to her underwear and fighting to get away.

The car pulled into the yard and parked behind the bound woman, casting an almost Christ-like shadow across the yard. Another figure stepped out of the car and stood in front of the headlights. He looked impossibly tall and from where Mackenzie stood, he seemed to not have a face. He paid the bound woman no mind and headed directly for the window. Mackenzie stood her ground, taking in more of the man's detail as he got closer to the window. His eyes were pitch-black and when he grinned at her, it seemed to stretch from ear to ear.

Mackenzie knew then that it was the Scarecrow Killer. More than that, it was the man that killed Susan Kellerman and Shanda Elliot. They were one and the same, the personification of the human corruption she had tried to understand since the night she walked in to discover the dead body of her father.

"Come get me," the dark figure said to her, placing an enormous and scarred hand on the window. The entire house seemed to rattle with the simple touch. *"I'm waiting..."*

Mackenzie took a step back and collided with something solid. She turned around and found her father there. He was standing up, his dead eyes looking down at her. He opened his mouth to speak to her and a strangled whisper came out.

"I'll always be dead, Mac," he said, reaching out to her. *"No matter how hard you fight, I'll always be dead."*

His hand fell on her shoulder and even through her shirt, she could feel that his dead flesh was impossibly cold.

"Daddy..." she said.

Mackenzie jerked awake at 4:32 and knew right away that she would not be going back to sleep. The tank top she wore to bed was soaked in sweat and her heart was hammering away in her chest. She got out of bed quickly, as if the bed itself had conjured the ghastly nightmare.

She took a shower and brewed a pot of coffee. She drank two cups while looking over the notes on the Kellerman and Elliot cases. She also made notes of her own concerning the suspect they'd apprehended at Dupont Circle Station and the fiber she'd spotted at the landfill.

Just before six, her phone dinged as she received a text message. She checked it and saw that the message was from Ellington:

You'll be getting an e-mail in the next few minutes that is going to sound scarier than it is. Remain calm. If you need to talk to someone when it's all said and done, reach out to me.

The message was cryptic beyond belief but she restrained herself from responding back with questions. She couldn't deny that the message made her terribly nervous, though. She looked at the third cup of coffee she had poured for herself and decided to pour it down the sink. She busied herself by getting dressed and fixing her hair, doing everything she could to not stress out about the way yesterday had ended and the alarming text from Ellington.

When she opened her mail on her phone twenty minutes after receiving Ellington's text, she found that she had a new mail waiting. It was from Deputy Director Justin McGrath, a man she had never met but had heard plenty about. Ultimately, he oversaw the bulk of active agents and their assignments. From what she understood, there were only one or two positions above him within the hierarchy of the Bureau.

Now more nervous than ever, she opened the e-mail. She found right away that the e-mail had been written by McGrath directly and not an assistant or secretary as most e-mails were from someone higher up. The message was plain, simple, and terrifying.

Ms. White,
It is crucial that you meet me in my office at 7:00 a.m. sharp. I have also made this same request of Agent Bryers.

She read the e-mail only once. That was all it took. There was no sign-off of any kind. Not a *thank you* or a *see you then.* Her nerves were like electric wires and a pit of worry formed in her stomach. If she had not already showered, she would have gone for a run just to relieve some tension. But she then recalled Ellington's text, telling her that there may be no real need to be scared.

Easier said than done, she thought as she headed out the door, wondering if this might be the last day she had to entertain the dream of becoming an agent.

CHAPTER SEVEN

Deputy Director McGrath's office was pristinely clean. The oak desk he sat behind gleamed in the morning sun that came in through the blinds. When Mackenzie walked into his office within the J. Edgar Hoover Building at 6:58, she saw that Bryers was already there. He was sitting in one of two chairs at one end of McGrath's desk. He looked like a man who knew he would soon be led to the gallows.

As for McGrath, he sat behind his desk with the authority of a bear in a cave. He was about the same age as Bryers but looked way more hardened. He wore a pair of eyeglasses that made him look almost villainous—which went well with the sour look he wore on his face.

"Shut the door behind you," McGrath ordered as she walked in.

Mackenzie did so and then walked to the other chair beside Bryers, where she sat down slowly. Before she had gotten fully seated, McGrath was on his feet and leering at both of them over the desk.

"I need one of you to explain how this whole scenario is going to work," he barked at them. "I was informed about our little experiment with Ms. White and thought it was stupid to begin with. But ultimately, the decision was made somewhere over my head and now I'm stuck dealing with your fuck-ups."

He focused solely on Mackenzie and when he did, his gaze fell on her like dead weight. "Make no mistake, Ms. White…I am not in favor of making people that have not even made it through the Academy feel special. I don't care if I hurt your feelings. I think having you on this case while just barely halfway through the Academy makes a laughingstock of the Bureau. On the other hand, I've read your dossier and heard your praises sung from more mouths than I care to admit. But this isn't shit-kicking country anymore, Ms. White. Do you understand that?"

"Yes, sir," she said.

"I'm not sure you do," he said. "If you did, then the suspect you two apprehended at the bus station last night would not have scrapes on his face and a bruise on his back the size of a grapefruit. If it weren't for the underhanded negotiations of Agent Bryers, the suspect could have easily lodged a complaint—a complaint that would have stuck, sending your ass packing back to Nebraska and making the people that made the decision to give you a shot look very stupid."

McGrath then turned his attention to Bryers, the vitriol and anger still present. "And *you* should have known better than to let her handle such a thing. What the hell were you thinking letting her run after the suspect?"

"I tried to tell her not to. But…she's damned fast, sir."

"I don't care how fast she is. You wanted a partner ASAP and this is the one you got. You agreed to this. So she's your responsibility. Understood?"

"Yes, sir."

"Did you hear that?" McGrath asked, looking back to Mackenzie. "You're his responsibility. You do *nothing* without his permission."

"Yes, sir."

McGrath took a deep breath and then removed his glasses. He massaged the area between his eyes with his thumb and forefinger, pushing a headache back before it was too far gone.

"I had a conversation with the other deputy directors, the section chiefs, and the director of the Bureau last night," McGrath said. "We took a vote and it was *really* close. For the sake of time and preventing any further murders, you are still on this case, Ms. White. However, if an arrest has not been made in forty-eight hours, you're off. And in that time, should you make any more stupid mistakes like you did last night, not only are you off the case, but you're also no longer a part of the Academy."

Mackenzie felt as if she had been slapped in the face. "Sir, that's—"

"If you end that statement with *not fair*, I'll see to it that you're done and headed back home *today*," he said.

Mackenzie snapped her mouth shut and did everything she could to hold his eye contact. As she did, he put his glasses back on and picked up a folder from his desk. He handed it to Bryers, seemingly happy to be rid of it.

"Hopefully, this will help," McGrath said. "These are the results from the sweep of the landfill fence last night. I received them less than an hour ago. There's a pretty solid lead here."

Bryers opened the folder, scanned it, and nodded. "Thank you, sir."

McGrath shrugged and opened his hands to them, palms outward. "Don't thank me. My hands are tied for the next forty-eight hours. Yours, however, are not. So I suggest both of you get out there and follow up on this right now."

Bryers got to his feet instantly. Mackenzie followed suit. They made their exit without McGrath saying another word.

When they started down the hall, which was starting to fill with the regular flow of morning workers, Bryers walked as close to her as he could. "You okay?" he asked.

"Yes," she said.

"Look…he's right. I shouldn't have let you rush after the guy."

"Forget it. What did we find out about him, anyway?"

"Nothing. He says he wasn't trying to offer the girl money for sex. But the guy has a record of petty theft and consensual sex with minors. We think he might be part of a small prostitution ring. He might have been trying to recruit the girl last night."

"Any link to Susan Kellerman?"

"Nothing obvious," he said. "But we've got a team working on it."

"And what about that folder?" she asked, nodding to the folder McGrath had just given him.

"Let's go find out," he said.

She nearly apologized for jumping the gun at the station last night, but bit it back. McGrath had just given her two days to help Bryers wrap this case up. Her career with the Bureau—her very future—was on the line now.

She wasn't about to waste time with apologies.

***

Mackenzie was looking at the file McGrath had given them while Bryers drove. The lead was for a man named Ronald Staunton, fifty-six. He currently worked as a gutter installer for a small construction company, with previous employment for a variety of other construction crews. He had been fired from at least three of his last jobs showing up to work drunk. The only dings he had on his criminal record were possession of marijuana from nearly fifteen years ago and a domestic abuse charge that had been thrown out in court.

As she looked through the folder, Bryers spoke up for the first time since they had hit the road. "One thing to remember about being an agent," he said, "is that it is *always* better to be safe than sorry. No one is ever going to scold you for being *too* thorough. And that's why I don't completely fault you for what you did last night. Sure, you were a little rough, but that happens from time to time. If FBI agents got their wrists slapped for every cut or bruise they inflicted on suspects during a chase or altercation, there wouldn't *be* a Bureau."

"I just…*acted*," Mackenzie said.

"I know what that's like," he said with a smile. "I can remember what it was like being an agent for that first year or so. I can only imagine what you're going through...not even out of the Academy yet. Anyway, I thought you should hear that. It looks like you lost some sleep over it. You look tired, Mackenzie."

"I am," she said.

"I don't sleep well sometimes either," he offered. "In this line of work, you see things you sometimes maybe shouldn't see. It starts to chip away at the way you sleep...hell, the way you *live*."

Mackenzie almost asked him what he meant. What had he seen or done during his time as an agent that had so deeply affected him? But she kept quiet; it was clear that he was done talking about it, as evidenced by his hard-set eyes and the way he made an effort to look forward, as if she was not in the car at all.

Ten minutes later, just as the dashboard clock ticked to 8:02, Bryers pulled the car to the side of the road along a modest residential street. Most people had not yet left for work, so the streets and driveways were filled with cars. As they parked, Mackenzie watched as a wife got into a clunker of a car four houses down. She was giving her two kids kisses goodbye as her husband watched from the front door.

"Anything in the file jump out at you?" Bryers asked. For now, he had apparently decided to slink back into the role of instructor.

"Nothing that aligns with a sudden interest in killing women," she answered. "The domestic abuse raises a flag but isn't a surefire accusation for murder. Based on what you told me, I think the guy from the station last night is a better fit."

"That's right. It's a shot in the dark, but—"

"But better safe than sorry," she said, echoing his earlier sentiment.

"That's exactly right."

They stepped out of the car together and made their way up Ronald Staunton's cracked concrete sidewalk. Bryers took the lead, ringing the doorbell and making sure to stand slightly in front of Mackenzie.

A dog started barking inside immediately. Mackenzie guessed it to be a mid-sized dog, possibly older. There was not much bite to its bark. Roughly ten seconds later, the front door was opened by a man who had crested middle age. He was wearing a white T-shirt and carpenter jeans. He was holding a cup of coffee as the barking dog—a crossbreed of a lab and beagle, it seemed—yammered on behind him. The man looked curiously at Mackenzie and Bryers while keeping the cowardly dog at bay with his right leg.

47

"It's early," the man said. "Can I help you?"

"Yes sir," Bryers said. "Are you Ronald Staunton?"

"I am. Again, can I help you?"

Bryers pulled his badge and ID out quickly, almost like a parlor trick. "I'm Agent Bryers, and this is Agent White," he said. "We'd like to ask you a few questions."

Staunton looked genuinely confused and the look that bloomed on his face when he saw the ID told Mackenzie all she needed to know: this was not their guy. Still, it wasn't her place to say anything just yet, so she let Bryers go through with it. She wasn't about to get in his way again.

"What about?" Staunton asked.

"Well, we'd like to know if you can provide your whereabouts over the course of the last few nights," Bryers said.

"Am I under arrest or something?" Staunton asked.

"No," Bryers said. "We just need to ask you some questions."

Staunton looked gravely at them for a moment. Mackenzie saw something very similar to disappointment in the man's eyes. Something about the way he looked at them was nearly heartbreaking.

"Look," Staunton said. "I made some mistakes in my past. I was a slob, I was lazy, and I was selfish. But I've turned myself around. Been sober for seven months and mended a lot of the bridges I thought I had burned. That old me...he was an asshole. That's not me anymore."

"That's fantastic," Bryers said genuinely. "All the same, we have a set of your fingerprints on a chain-link fence from a landfill where two bodies have recently been dumped. More than that, we also have a white fiber that we believe is from a shirt. We are currently having DNA tests run on the fabric and believe it will also point directly to you."

"Bodies?" Staunton said, aghast. "Murder? Are you for real? I hit my wife in a drunken act of stupidity six years ago and that's enough to flag me for a murder suspect?"

"When your prints are found at the scene of where a body was discovered, yes, it does."

"Ah, hell," Staunton said, slapping his hand against the doorframe in frustration. "You know what? Fine. Yes. I climbed over a fence at the landfill three nights ago. But all I was doing was getting rid of paint cans for the guy I'm working with. We can't dump them anywhere because environment freaks are all worried about paint hurting the earth or whatever. So yeah...I did that. I've done it a few times."

"You have proof?" Bryers asked.

"No. Not unless my employer wants to fess up to illegal dumping."

"Can we please come in?" Bryers asked. "This shouldn't take too long."

"And what if I say no?" Staunton asked.

"Sir," Mackenzie said, sincerely feeling bad for him, "there's no need to make this harder than it is. If you say no, we'll go get a warrant and be back in a few hours and go through this again. If we have to, we'll come to your work and show you the warrant. Or you could just invite is in now."

"Fine," Staunton said, stepping aside, kicking the dog back lightly as he did so. "Come in and ask your questions. It's a damn shame that the idea that someone can truly change isn't worth a cup of piss anymore, isn't it?"

Mackenzie and Bryers headed inside, silent because there was nothing either of them could say to that.

There was nothing more to do here, anyway, Mackenzie realized. A guilty man, no matter how good of an actor, would have at least a trace of fear in that first initial moment. Staunton looked genuinely shocked, though.

She sighed, knowing this wasn't their man.

The real killer, though, was out there somewhere.

And the clock was ticking.

CHAPTER EIGHT

His mother was in her bedroom, watching one of her stupid morning game shows. Her bedroom was in the back of the house, off in the farthest corner, and the noise filled the rest of the house like a muted explosion. She'd laugh every now and then, laughter that would morph into her loud, dry coughs. The sound was like nails on a chalkboard to him. Every time he heard it, he wished she'd die. Maybe he'd finally get the courage to kill her in her sleep—to place a pillow over her stupid fat face or to just hold his strong hands over her nose and mouth and watch her suffocate.

It had nothing to do with a lack of courage, though. He had all the courage in the world. What it came down to was that he loved her. He loved his mother very much; she just got annoying and extremely inconvenient at times.

It was one of the reasons he was glad to have the mangy old addition on the back of the house. He'd built it himself, taking about two weeks to create the two-room domicile that was attached to the rear walkway of his mother's house. Even at twenty-three years of age, almost two decades ago, done with college and with no real job prospects, he'd known that his mother would need him. Someone had to take care of her and she sure as hell wasn't going to find a man to spend the rest of her life with. She was three hundred and forty pounds and, quite simply, didn't care. She could die tomorrow, but as long as she did it while drinking her sodas and inhaling a box of oatmeal crème pies, she'd be fine with her demise.

He had just finished cleaning the living room, prepared to head back to his little add-on dwelling where he'd probably spend a few hours online doing absolutely nothing, when he spotted movement through the living room blinds. He peered through the slats and saw a man walking up the sidewalk. He was carrying a large book under his arm and was dressed in a button-down short-sleeve shirt and a pair of khakis. A pair of eyeglasses clung to his nose and ears, making his face appear thin.

"Hey, Ma!" he shouted.

He heard no response, just the blaring of the television from her corner of the house. Quickly, he walked to the hallway and took a few steps toward his room.

"Ma!"

After a moment, the TV went silent. They did this sort of back and forth several times a day. He knew that she was muting the show, probably annoyed. Then her voice came at him through the thin walls. It was thick and garbled, the sound of a lazy fallen animal that has given up on the hunt.

"What?" she bellowed.

"Did you make an appointment with another one of those salespeople for today?"

There was a moment as she thought about this but then she answered: "That's for Saturday! I'm not expecting anyone today!"

His mother tended to make appointments with salespeople on a regular basis. It was why they had more kitchen knives than they'd ever use. It was why his mother had tons of makeup, smoothie solutions, and weight loss gimmicks piled in the closet that had only ever been used once—if at all. The woman had no life and hated to leave the house. *No use going out into the world when the world can come to you,* she had told him on more than one occasion.

He felt the same way…only not in regards to shopping.

"Okay," he bellowed back.

The noise of her daytime game show came back in full force. It made him turn his hands into fists. Not only was she slowly eating herself to death but the bitch was apparently losing her hearing, too.

Several moments later, the man he had spied coming up the walk knocked on the front door. Not wanting to seem too excited, he waited a moment before answering the door. He felt his heartbeat growing in his chest, his palms getting sweaty, and the beginnings of an erection in the front of his pants.

Slowly, he advanced toward the front door. He opened it, putting on his best look of disinterest. It was important to get the expression just right; he didn't want to look *too* disinterested. He wanted them to think they had a chance to sell whatever crap they were peddling. Now that the salesman was at the door, he saw that it was not a plain book under the man's arm, but a large binder. The company name along the spine read THE GREEN TEAM LAWN CARE.

"Hey there," the bespectacled man said. "My name is Trevor Simms and I'm one of the soil techs with the Green Team. Have you heard of us, by any chance?"

"I actually haven't," he responded.

"Well, what we do," Trevor said, "is make sure your lawn looks the best it can for the lowest cost. Now, I noticed some dead spots out front and we can take care of that for you. There are also a lot of weeds around the sides and—"

"Let me cut you off right there, Trevor," he said. "Living in this neighborhood, do you really think I can afford to have someone fix my yard? Spending money on making my grass look pretty is not high on my list of priorities."

Undaunted, Trevor went on. "Oh, I hear that. Trust me, I do. But with our prices, you'd be surprised at just what you can do to make your yard look perfectly green."

He waited a while before answering. He even made an effort to pretend like he was looking over Trevor Simms's shoulder to see the dead grass in question. "Ah, hell," he said. "Come on in...Trevor, was it?"

"That's right," Trevor said, stepping inside. "You're making a great decision."

"Oh, I haven't decided anything yet," he said.

He heard the television blaring through the walls. It was almost as loud as the voices he sometimes heard at night...the voices from the foot of his bed. He thought he heard them now, through the noise of his mother's fucking television shows. He also felt a familiar headache coming on and he knew what had to be done to make it go away.

So in that moment, he *did* make a decision, although it had nothing at all to do with lawn care. In fact, he was already thinking about shoving this four-eyed imbecile into the crawlspace in his small addition to his mother's house.

"Have a seat, Trevor," he said, closing the door behind them. "Let's have a talk, you and I."

CHAPTER NINE

That afternoon, Mackenzie found herself walking a little too slowly toward a bar called Red's Roost. She'd been there only once before, during her first week in Quantico, where she had sadly nursed a mojito by herself. Now she looked to the place with a new sort of fear—a creeping unease that she knew she should listen to but was bucking up against for reasons she didn't understand.

She walked inside, passed by the hostess with a little smile and a wave, and headed straight for the bar. When her eyes fell on Ellington, that unease shifted in her gut and felt like a lead weight. She should not be here. She should not be doing this. Even though Ellington insisted there was nothing more than career interest here and she *did* believe it, there was still something wrong about it.

He waved to her and playfully patted the back of the seat beside him. She walked over and was glad to see the bar was packed. There was absolutely no chance at all that this was going to turn into anything intimate or inappropriate.

You're making too big of a deal about your own self, she thought as she sat down across from Ellington. *He doesn't think of you like that. You're just the poor stranded girl from Nebraska that he's trying to help get a pair of solid feet beneath. Why are you trying to ruin it?*

She had no idea. What she *did* know, though, was that she was nervous around him in a way that made her feel off of her game but, at the same time, like a delighted high school girl.

"Tough day?" he asked.

"I've had better," she said. "Thanks for the heads-up about the meeting with McGrath."

"Sure. I heard about the crap deal. Forty-eight hours, huh?"

"Well, technically, I'm down to just thirty-eight now. So…no offense, can we get to the point of you asking me here?"

A waitress came by, breaking up the back-and-forth. They ordered their drinks (a stout for Ellington and a martini for her) and she waited to see where Ellington would take the conversation. He had been the one to request this little meeting for drinks, so she'd be damned if she'd muck it all up by forcing small talk—especially not when her career was ticking away with every breath. She got the sense that Ellington was also not a fan of small talk; it was one of the things she liked about him.

"So," he finally said, "word of your recruitment has gotten out to your fellow classmates somehow."

"How?" she asked.

"No idea. Even in the FBI, gossip can be a killer. However, no one knew about the recruitment other than Bryers, you, me, and the deputy directors. The best we can figure, someone maybe overheard some of the conversation we had over coffee when we approached you."

"So is everyone pissed at me now?" Mackenzie asked.

"Pissed? No. Jealous…maybe. But your past is heralded even among your classmates. I think they understand. But still…like gossip, jealousy is also a sad reality to working your way up through the Bureau. I don't think anyone knows about the ridiculous timeline that McGrath strapped you with, though."

"Ah, so I'm being thrust back into the social structure of high school again."

Ellington smirked at her. "Is it any worse than where you came from?"

She thought of Porter and Nelson back in Nebraska. Although Porter had come around before she'd left, the entire experience had left a bad taste in her mouth. "Touché," she said, followed by a sip from her martini.

"But, speaking of where you came from," Ellington said, "I must admit, I am here solely as a friend."

"Oh?" she asked.

"Yeah. The directors are still trying to figure it all out. There's talk about how it might have been a mistake to try this experiment at all. They wonder if you've undergone a proper psych evaluation. After the Scarecrow Killer case, you're considered *at risk* in terms of your mental state."

She bit back a smile. She *had* seen a shrink during her first two weeks in Quantico—two quick sessions that had been suggested by Ellington and her assistant director. But the sessions had not been mandatory and she'd given up on them after two weeks. She'd made the Academy her priority and her psychological well-being had gone by the wayside.

"I'm fine," she said. "No dark thoughts. No nightmares." Only when she said the word *nightmares*, her blood went cold. The image of the Scarecrow Killer in her childhood front yard and backing into the rotting arms of her dead father flashed across the eye of her mind and then disappeared.

"Would you tell me otherwise?" he asked.

"No."

"Well, at least you're honest. But look…if you feel like we threw you into the deep end without asking if you could swim, you have to let me know now rather than later."

"I'm fine, Ellington. And besides, in thirty-eight hours, it could all be over anyway."

He smiled at her and they locked eyes for a moment. She looked away, reminding herself that he was married and that he had already shot down her advances once.

"Don't let him know I told you this," Ellington said, "but Bryers thinks you're awesome. He gushed about your dossier before he even met you. He's nervous because of the responsibility, but he's glad to have you."

Mackenzie wasn't sure how to respond, so she simply took another gulp from her drink. It felt good going down and she couldn't help but wonder what it might be like to sit here with this interesting man and get pretty close to drunk again. Maybe this time, the result would be different.

It doesn't change the fact that he's married, she thought.

"What's the deal with Bryers anyway?" Mackenzie asked.

"What do you mean?"

"Well, he's all about asking questions about my past, which is good. It shows that he's interested. But whenever I ask him even the smallest question about his past, he clams up."

Bryers nodded. "Yeah, that's Bryers. I've known him for about six years now and he's a pretty closed book. I haven't pried, but I hear he was involved in a case a while back that sort of messed him up. Something to do with a kidnapping case gone really bad. He had to take some time off. So…just don't pry too much."

"I won't."

The table fell into silence again and Mackenzie was very aware of the way he was looking at her. It was very different from the brief time they had spent together in Nebraska. It was the same way Zack had once looked at her back when they had started dating—a look that had grown dimmer and dimmer the longer they had stayed together.

Harry Dougan looked at her like that from time to time as well. She wondered how he would feel if he knew she was having this little meeting with Ellington.

"So how are things going with you?" she asked.

"Decent, I guess. I'm heading up this domestic terrorism task force. It's almost a desk job, really. But it's high-speed, you know? I've been pulling eighty-hour weeks for the last month."

"That sounds exciting."

"Sure it is. And tiring. It also tends to piss spouses off."

"I'm sure."

She noticed him sliding his index finger around the surface of his wedding ring. He opened his mouth to say something and then seemed to think better of it.

"What is it?" she asked.

"Nothing you want to hear," Ellington said.

"Probably not," Mackenzie said. "But I asked anyway, didn't I?"

He hesitated for a moment, taking a long pull from his beer. When he set it back down, his tone seemed to have changed. "This job," he said. "It's rewarding, fun as hell, and exciting. But if you picked any five married people at random—male or female—from the Bureau, I can guarantee you that at least three have troubled marriages or have been divorced at least once. With this job, you marry it. It becomes your life, you know?"

She nodded. She'd heard such things before, especially during the introductory courses she'd sat through when she first arrived in Quantico. Maybe that's why she was so drawn to it; it took the place of fostering any sort of relationships with people.

"My wife is just about done," he said. "If it wasn't for our kid, I'm pretty sure she'd be gone by now."

A million clichéd phrases went through Mackenzie's head, but she ended up opting for "I'm sorry to hear it."

"The hell of it is that if she *made* me choose between her and the job, she'd be packing her things pretty quickly. It kills me to admit that, but it's the truth."

That comment left the table in silence again. Things had suddenly gotten awkward and she could tell that Ellington sensed that he had maybe gone too far. Mackenzie started looking for excuses to leave, any reason to remove herself from a situation she wasn't sure she'd be able to defuse if it went too far. As it turned out, though, she didn't need an excuse. Her phone rang in the midst of the silence and she answered it right away. She gave Ellington an apologetic glance as she answered.

"Hello?" she asked.

"Hey," came Bryers's voice from the other end of the line. It sounded somber and quiet. She wondered, rather selfishly, if McGrath had talked the other directors into cutting her loose right now rather than two days from now.

"We've got a third body."

Mackenzie felt her heart pounding in her chest as he gave her directions to the new dump, barely hearing him. She felt waves of guilt for being unable to stop the killer in time. She knew this was too fast for three bodies; the stakes had been upped dramatically and everything was about to change.

She paused as she got up from the table and looked back to Ellington as she downed her drink.

"Another body?" he guessed.

She nodded back, sharing his somber glance.

"I hope things get patched up with your wife. In the meantime, maybe you shouldn't have drinks with the young lady recruit that came on to you that one time in Nebraska."

He nodded, grim, whether from the body or her statement, she could not tell.

"Yeah, maybe not."

With that, Mackenzie turned away from him and headed back outside, where the night seemed a little darker after having received Bryers's call.

CHAPTER TEN

When Mackenzie arrived at the dump, a small team of agents was already there. They had blocked off the entrance to the dump even though it was after operating hours. Behind the two cars and single agent that were blocking the entrance, a crew was setting up miniature floodlights to illuminate the grounds.

She stopped her car at the car-barricade. A young agent stepped forward and she rolled down her window. When he looked inside at her, she could sense right away that he was new. All new agents seemed to have a certain fake-hardened look to them, like they were trying a little too hard.

God, don't let me become one of those types, she thought.

"This landfill is a restricted area right now, ma'am," the agent said.

"I know," Mackenzie said. "I'm Mackenzie White. Agent Bryers should have called ahead for me."

The agent nodded and gave her a quick smile. Behind it, she thought she saw a trace of resentment. "He sure did. Can I see some ID?"

It occurred to her then that all she had in the form of ID were her driver's license and her Academy ID card. She showed the agent both, feeling like a novice for not being able to present an actual badge or, at the very least, a temporary ID card on a lanyard or something. Satisfied, the agent allowed her to park her car. She then got out and walked up the slight incline to the flat area where the floodlights were being set up.

As she did, she heard the agent behind her at the barricade speak in not quite a whisper into a hand-held radio. "Mackenzie White is on the scene."

Following this, every figure up ahead by the lights and the edge of the dump turned to regard her. She felt like a bug under a microscope as she approached the dumps and wondered if she should have waited for Bryers before getting out of the car.

There were five huge green dumps sitting at the edge of a big paved ramp, much like the last dump. It was easy to peer into the tops of them, as the bottoms were recessed through the pavement and sitting on the ground by the exit road that led away from the dump. Mackenzie looked inside each one of them, scanning.

She saw the body in the third dump. It was lying on its side, naked. The leg hair alone made it clear that it was indeed a male. From where she stood, she could see nothing to indicate the cause of death. She turned to the men putting up the lights and was about to ask them when she saw a set of headlights approaching. A few others followed behind the first pair.

She walked down the small ramp, back past the barricade, and watched as the new vehicles parked. There three in all: two sedans and one SUV. They all had government plates.

Bryers stepped out of the first car and hurried over to her. "Sorry I'm late," he said. "I had to scramble to get out of the office and assemble this team." He hitched a thumb over his shoulder as he said this last bit.

"It's okay," she said.

"You see the body?"

"Yeah. It's in the center bin."

Bryers thought about something for a moment and gave her a sincere look. Behind him, several people were hopping out of the SUV and the other cars. They spoke to one another quietly and moved efficiently in the dark.

"Listen," Bryers said. "Things are going to move fast for the next half an hour or so. I want you here, but I also want you to sort of stand back behind it all. Watch closely and take mental notes. If you see something someone misses, don't say anything right away. When the body is out and the crowd disperses, let me know of any questions or comments you have. Is that okay with you?"

"Yes, I can do that." She was pleased to see that any anger he had toward her yesterday was gone. He was back to being a partner—maybe even a mentor of a sort.

"Great," he said, looking up the ramp to the where spotlights were now secured and shining down on the crime scene. "You ready?"

She could only nod as she followed behind him and walked back up toward the dumps.

The coroner arrived ten minutes later. By then, two agents had climbed over into the large green garbage bin to inspect the body. Mackenzie had done as Bryers had asked, standing behind the commotion and watching. She overheard most of the conversations and picked up several bits of information which she mentally filed away.

There was a large bruise in the center of the man's chest that was likely a hematoma—meaning he had been hit hard there. There were other bruises and a single stab wound along the man's stomach, but there appeared to be very little blood. Several of the man's fingernails were torn and there appeared to be scratches and scuff marks along most of his fingers. He had a tattoo on his upper back, along the right shoulder, of what appeared to be a small dragon.

The man was out of the bin moments later and placed on a stretcher. Before the coroner moved the body, Bryers stepped forward. "Hey, guys, give me two minutes before you take the body, would you?"

The men nodded, looking very anxious to get out of the too-bright glow of the small floodlights. Bryers looked to Mackenzie and waved her over. She went quickly, not realizing until she got there that she had never seen a dead male this close up in her line of work. The Scarecrow Killer had caused her to see three dead women, but this was the first naked male form she'd been asked to look at.

"Look him over," Bryers said. "Don't touch anything. Just give him a once-over and let me know what you see."

She bent down to better observe the body. Bryers handed her a small Maglite and stepped back, giving her some room. The dump went quiet but she barely noticed. She slipped into a focus that she only ever experienced when deeply into her work.

"I assume there was blunt-force trauma to the chest," she said. "The condition of his hands and fingers—including the torn fingernails—indicates that he was likely trapped before he was killed. There's noticeable dirt under his nails—pale in color. It's loose dirt, not packed." She leaned in closer and observed the lacerations on his fingers. "I'd guess there was some sort of rough surface, too. Wood maybe."

She kept looking and came to his knees. "Slight abrasions on his knees, looks almost like slight rug burn or maybe the same material that damaged his fingernails. Redness around the area indicates that it was recent. No more than a day and a half or so for sure. He was on his knees at some point in the last thirty-six hours, maybe crawling."

She looked back to Bryers and saw that he was nodding with enthusiasm. "Go on. Keep going."

She didn't think there was anything else of note until she had nearly given up. The added pressure of everyone watching her made her feel like she had to find something. When she reached the man's head, she saw something that she at first dismissed as garbage. She leaned forward and examined the substance in the man's hair with the flashlight.

"Can I see a pen or something?" she asked.

Bryers was there right away, handing her a pen. She used it to softly brush at the man's hair. The substance in his hair looked like powder at first but then the light hit it in a particular way and revealed something else.

"What is that?" someone asked from behind her. Apparently, it was something they had missed.

"Just something from the garbage," someone answered dismissively.

"No," Mackenzie said. "It's fluffy. It looks like...some sort of insulation." She scraped a small piece of it from the man's head with the pen and picked it up from the pavement. She rolled it between her fingers and nodded. "Yeah...insulation."

She handed it up to Bryers and when he took it, he looked almost happy. As juvenile as it made her feel, she sort of hoped it was because her discovery had impressed him.

Mackenzie looked through the man's hair a bit longer and felt connections starting to form. She saw more pale dirt in the man's hair, the same dirt that was under his nails. More than that, though, she saw a small bloody gash hidden under his hair. She pushed the hair back with the pen and leaned back so the others could see it.

"A small gash here," she said. "Sort of raw, so definitely recent just like the other minor wounds. About an inch in diameter, but pretty deep. Looks haphazard, not intentional."

She handed the pen back to Bryers, who instantly tossed it into the nearest bin. When she got to her feet, done with her examination, the body was moved away from the bins and down to the coroner's vehicle.

The group of agents and consultants broke up and departed just as quickly as they had come. Bryers, on the other hand, seemed not to be in any hurry. As they walked down to their cars, he looked out to the highway, a dark stretch of nothing about three hundred yards away from the dump exit. Headlights came and went, as small as little insects from this distance.

"That was impressive," Bryers said. "If you hadn't seen that cut in his head, it would have gone unnoticed until he got put on the coroner's table."

"I'm not sure how much help such a small find will do."

"Honestly, for now, that find alone will probably do nothing. But why don't you tell me what you think it means?"

She was hesitant at first, not wanting to be wrong. But everything in her gut told her that she was either right or close to it—close enough to narrow their search, anyway.

"Dirt in his hair and slightly damaged knees indicate that he was crawling. Add that with the horrible state of his hands, and not only was he crawling, but he was trying to escape...maybe from somewhere he felt he actually had a chance of escaping. It makes me think that he was being held somewhere before he was brought here—maybe a cage outdoors or something, like a kennel."

"Okay, let's consider that," Bryers said. "But if that's the case, what about the accidental gouge on his head?"

"Well," she said, thinking out loud now. "If he was on his hands and knees, crawling and trying to get out of something, I think that puncture wound came from something over his head. Probably a nail. So maybe a very low ceiling."

"So you're thinking a cage?" Bryers asked.

"Or some kind of box."

Silence fell between them as they both thought this over. They could hear the muted noises of passing cars on the highway on the other side of the landfill.

"Maybe not a *box* per se," Bryers said. "Maybe we're looking for something like a cutaway section of floor. Maybe a crawlspace."

"Maybe," Mackenzie said, thinking he was exactly right.

"Well, the night is far from over," Bryers said. "We'll get an ID on the body within an hour. After that, the family will be notified and we'll have to talk to them. How do you feel about taking the lead on that? Let me sit back and watch this time."

"That's fine," she said.

"Now, given that you're running out of time to bundle this thing up, what do you think comes next? We can either head back to headquarters and pretend that we can contribute to paperwork, or grab a burger at this amazing little dive down the street."

Neither avenue sounded very productive, although restudying the paperwork for clues about the nature of the killer sounded appealing to her. But she also knew that she had been given a golden opportunity and that time was running out. Staying closer to the scene of the crime would probably end up working in their favor.

"I'd like to stick around here," she said. "See if we can find anything else noteworthy."

"Sounds good," he said.

Behind them, the other agents and consultants were already packing up to go. It was a stark reminder of how quickly everything moved in a case like this. Fifteen minutes ago, this landfill had been awash in floodlights and cramped with government employees. Now it was eerily quiet and back to natural darkness.

Thinking this, Mackenzie knew that she also needed to act fast. The speed and accuracy she displayed in the next few days could very well make or break her future.

CHAPTER ELEVEN

Mackenzie had barely been scouring the site for ten minutes when Bryers received a call. Not only had the body of the dead man been identified as Trevor Simms, a father of two and married for ten years, but the family had already been notified. They were obviously devastated but they were also eager to speak to someone who might be able to find out what had happened.

They got into Bryers's car, Mackenzie taking the wheel, and sped to the Simms residence. While they made the drive fifteen minutes south of Quantico, Bryers tended to several e-mails and calls regarding the case. As they got closer to the Simms residence, they received more information; bit by bit, Mackenzie started to make connections and was slowly able to form some sort of shape out of the chaos.

"Okay, so here's where we stand," Bryers said, reading over the last e-mail that had come in. "Trevor Simms, age thirty-one, married with two kids. He was co-owner of a small lawn care business that netted less than forty grand last year. Upstanding guy, it looks like. Coached his daughter's softball team and mowed his church's lawn on Saturday afternoons. His wife is Colette, thirty-three, a nurse at Stafford Hospital. Neither of them have a criminal record and it even looks like Trevor volunteered with the fire department for a few years."

"So no enemies," Mackenzie said.

"Not looking like it. Makes me think the victims this guy is picking are random."

"That makes this a lot harder, doesn't it?" Mackenzie said.

"Yeah. Nineteen times out of twenty, if you can come up with motive, you can nab your killer in less than a week. Without motive or reasoning, though, it's just a guessing game."

Mackenzie hated guessing. She even hated any sort of game where guessing was involved. She needed logic; she needed facts. So getting such detailed information on the victim so quickly made her think they were being more productive than Bryers was giving them credit for.

They arrived at the Simmses house eight minutes later, at 10:18 p.m. There was no trace of a police presence, making Mackenzie wonder if they'd be the first people to speak with the wife other than the officer or agent that had suffered the unfortunate duty of telling her that her husband was dead. She'd been in those shoes a

63

few times before while working for the police and she knew that it was emotionally draining.

They got out of the car and headed up the small front porch of the Simmses' cute two-story house. The siding was in need of a wash and the paint on the porch was cracking. A few toys were on the porch, as well as two rocking chairs. It was rustic and charming—the sort of home shared by a couple that likely paid their bills on time with very little to spend afterward.

She rang the bell, taking the lead as Bryers had suggested earlier. Right away, they could hear the shuffling of footsteps as someone came rushing to the door. Seconds later, a blonde woman in her early thirties answered. Her eyes were puffy and red and she looked exhausted—both physically and emotionally. Mackenzie wondered how much time had passed between getting the visit informing her that her husband was dead and having two agents show up at her door to ask her questions. Surely no more than three hours.

Mackenzie gave Colette Simms all the credit in the world. She did her absolute best to look like she was holding it together when she greeted them. She wondered if the recent widow had really started to grasp the totality of what had happened.

"You're the agents?" she asked. Her voice was hoarse from screaming and weeping.

"Yes, we are," Mackenzie said. "I'm Agent White, and this is Agent Bryers. We certainly appreciate you taking the time to speak with us."

Colette nodded and fought back tears. "The agent I spoke with on the phone said the faster you could speak to me, the better chance we have to uncovering something about the person that k—k—killed him."

She broke there, having to voice the fact that someone had killed her husband. She half-fell against the wall and let out a sob. Mackenzie didn't miss a beat; she didn't even look at Bryers for any sort of approval. She simply stepped inside the front door and placed a reassuring arm around Colette Simms.

She said nothing, letting Colette collapse into her arms and sob. Mackenzie looked to Bryers and he nodded at her. He looked a little uneasy but he also came into the house. He quietly shut the door behind him and slowly walked around them, into a small foyer.

"I'm…I'm so sorry," Colette said between hitching breaths. "It's still not…sinking in…"

"I know," Mackenzie said. "I'm so sorry."

"The kids…I had to call my mother to come get them. They still don't know…they're so young and—"

"Well, Mrs. Simms," Mackenzie said, "for right now, let's let them not know, okay? For right now, I really need to speak with you. Like that other agent told you, the sooner we can speak with you, the better our chances are of finding out who did this. Did the agent you spoke with tell you that there have been others?"

She nodded. "Young girls in dumps."

"That's right. So it's looking like we have a serial killer on our hands. And you could help us stop him before he kills again. You could get answers not only about Trevor, but about the two young women that have also died."

Colette nodded slowly. She started crying again but this time they were stray tears that poured over the corners of her eyes. She sniffed a few sobs back and when she sat down on the couch and relaxed, Mackenzie took this as the best moment to question her.

"Do you have any idea what Trevor's day looked like yesterday?" Mackenzie asked.

"Most of the past week or so, he and Benjamin were trying to drum up new business."

"Who is Benjamin?"

"The co-owner of their business. The Green Team. They did lawn care and restoration."

"And does Benjamin know what has happened?" Mackenzie asked.

"Ah, God, no. I haven't told him yet. I didn't even think—"

She paused here and Mackenzie sensed another meltdown coming. Again, though, Colette showed her strength and swallowed it down, focused on the task at hand.

"That's okay," Mackenzie said when she saw that Colette had control again. "Had business been bad lately?"

"Not bad, really. Just slow. It had never been a very successful business. But he also did some mechanic work on the side and it helped a lot."

"Do you know of any enemies Trevor might have had?" Mackenzie asked. "Any clients that were hostile?"

Colette smiled and started sniffing again. She grabbed a tissue from a nearby box and wiped at her puffy eyes. "No, no enemies. In fact, I don't think I ever heard Trevor utter a truly mean word against anyone. He had so many friends…one of the good guys, you know? Always helping others and even *looking* for ways to help people." She paused here and there was a frown on her face as she thought about something.

"What is it?" Mackenzie asked.

"Well, last year, Trevor worked on a guy's truck and ended up not being able to fix it. Even Trevor said he did more harm than good. It ended up costing the guy about five hundred dollars in the long run. Trevor paid it off eventually but before that, the guy got furious. He came to the house, went into the little garage Trevor has out back, and assaulted him. It was nothing serious, just a single punch. But then he started throwing around some of Trevor's equipment."

"Do you remember this man's name?"

"Lonnie Smith."

"Did you ever see him after that?" Bryers asked.

"No. Trevor spent three months paying him back and after that, we severed ties."

Mackenzie thought about this for a moment and then went on. "You said you think Trevor had been trying to drum up business for the last few weeks. Do you know what that entailed?"

She felt Bryers behind her, slowly scanning the room. She felt like he was monitoring her, as if she was taking some weird sort of real-life exam. She didn't mind, actually. She understood the line of thought. More than that, it made her more aware of every question that came out of her mouth.

"They did a few different things, actually," Colette said. "A lot of it was calling clients from the past. They also spent some money on targeted online ads and ran Facebook campaigns. Things like that. When times got really tough last year, they even went so far as to drive the company truck through different neighborhoods, going door to door."

Mackenzie looked back to Bryers. An *a-ha* moment bloomed between them and Colette Simms barely noticed. She looked deep in thought, staring at the kitchen wall across from them. "I really should tell Benjamin," she said.

"Mrs. Simms," Mackenzie said. "Do you know if they had been doing the door-to-door approach this week?"

"I don't know," Collette said absently. Mackenzie noticed that Colette seemed to be slipping away from them. It was all too much for her; it made Mackenzie feel guilty for questioning her so soon.

She walked over to Bryers and leaned in close. "We need to get an officer over here to sit with her while someone else gets her family affairs in order. She's fading fast…and when she snaps out of whatever fugue she's slipping into, it's going to be nasty."

Bryers nodded. "Absolutely. You wrap things up with her and I'll make some calls."

"Maybe see what you can do to find out some more information on Lonnie Smith, too," Mackenzie suggested. She felt awkward giving Bryers instructions, but he didn't seem to mind.

Mackenzie went back to Colette Simms. She sat down on the couch beside her and, after some hesitation, reached out and took her hand.

"Thank you, Mrs. Simms. You've been a great help. We'll have someone here soon to help you with everything."

Colette only nodded. She still stared toward the far kitchen wall on the other side of the house. "It makes no sense," she said. Her voice sounded like someone was talking in their sleep. "Who would do such a thing to Trevor? He never got involved with anything bad...never got into any trouble. He didn't deserve this..."

She went quiet then and Mackenzie watched a single tear roll down the side of her face. She heard Bryers speaking on the phone in the foyer and wondered if the information Colette had provided had struck him the same way it had struck her.

Susan Kellerman had been going door to door with her health products.

There was a very good chance that Trevor Simms had been going door to door trying to drum up business for his lawn care company.

And then there was the last thing Colette had told her. *He never got involved with anything bad...never got into any trouble.*

Maybe the killer wasn't having to hunt down his victims.

Perhaps the victims were going right to him.

CHAPTER TWELVE

As they walked back down Colette Simms's front porch, Mackenzie was anxious to share her theory. More than that, she was certain there would be a very easy clue to help them along—a dead giveaway that could help them locate the killer to within an area of a few blocks. She opened her mouth to share all of this when Bryers's phone rang.

She listened to his end of the conversation as they got into the car. All she heard was a series of *yeah* and *uh-huh* as she got behind the wheel and backed out of the driveway. Bryers gave a final *yeah* to the person on the other end and then hung up. He looked directly at Mackenzie and smiled.

"You ready for this?" Bryers asked.

"What?"

"We got information on Lonnie Smith."

"Already?" Mackenzie asked, genuinely shocked at the speed of information.

"Already," Bryers confirmed. "Not only does he have a criminal record, but it includes a nine-month stint in prison for attempted kidnapping five years ago. Want to guess where he was busted?"

"Near Dupont Circle Station?"

"Bingo."

The connection was so astounding that it made her grin. She could feel a growing excitement blossoming between them but she tried to keep it suppressed for now. The last thing she wanted to do was get overzealous.

"Okay, but what about the door-to-door connection?" she asked. "That can't just be coincidence, right?"

"You picked up on that, too, huh?" Bryers asked.

"It's sort of hard not to."

"I don't know," Bryers said thoughtfully. "I've seen stranger coincidences." He hesitated for a moment and then frowned. It nearly killed the growing excitement between them completely.

"What?" she asked.

"You think Lonnie Smith is a dead-end, don't you?" he asked. "Already?"

"I wouldn't go *that* far," she said. "Given the circumstances, I think it's certainly worth looking into for sure."

"But you're more sold on a door-to-door connection?"

"Yes. And you know, there's an easy way to find out."

"Yeah? Like what?"

"Well, Colette told us that they would take the company truck out to different neighborhoods, looking for new clients. And if Trevor was abducted and never made it back to his truck…"

"Then there's a very obvious clue sitting on the side of the street, probably with a Green Team decal on its doors," Bryers finished.

"Potentially. I think it would also be beneficial to speak with his co-worker to find out what neighborhoods they visited this week."

"Two leads from one visit," Bryers said. "I like results like that."

"Okay then," Mackenzie said. "Where first?"

"Well, both and neither. I have Lonnie Smith's address, and we can visit him in the morning. Potential suspects are going to be more cooperative after having woken up—not after being jarred awake just before midnight. He lives about forty minutes from the Academy, so we'll leave early in the morning. Not too early, though; tomorrow is Saturday after all. In the meantime, I'll make a call and see what I can do about getting an agent or maybe even just local PD to speak with the Green Team co-owner to see if we can find out where Trevor was trying to drum up business yesterday. When we have a location, maybe we can get a few cars to run a circuit of about five miles around the area, looking for a Green Team truck. And just in case it's not a clearly marked truck, I'll get Trevor Simms's license plate number, too."

"Sounds good," Mackenzie said.

"It does," Bryers said. "But of course, you know better than to get your hopes up until there's an actual verified suspect in custody, right?"

"Yes, I know."

He nodded satisfactorily and headed back out into the night, leaving behind a house that contained a grieving spouse for the second time in two days.

CHAPTER THIRTEEN

The following morning, Mackenzie met Bryers in the Academy parking lot with a hot cup of coffee waiting. This time, he had a temporary badge for her, a plastic card attached to a lanyard that she placed around her neck.

"I pushed for them to just let you have the real thing," he said. "They wouldn't do it. Apparently, they take their badges pretty seriously."

"And what would be the point?" Mackenzie asked. "After all, I'm only going to be around for another twenty-eight hours."

She could see that Bryers was trying to think of something reassuring to say but was at a loss. Not giving things a chance to get awkward, Mackenzie got into their car and waited for him to do the same. It made her think of how Ellington had told her about something Bryers had encountered in his past related to work that had altered him somehow. Even now, after working with him for the better part of two says, Mackenzie still wasn't quite sure what sort of personality he had.

It was 7:05 when they pulled out of the parking lot. They barely got ahead of morning rush hour traffic—another thing it was taking her some time to get used to about the area around DC. Even on a Saturday morning, the ride in traffic was intimidating.

"So we're coordinating with Quantico and Washington DC PD," Bryers said. "Benjamin Worley, the other Green Team guy, gave us two locations Trevor was assigned to yesterday, all within a mile of one another. They have a few cars canvassing one neighborhood in particular where quite a bit of criminal activity is usually reported. All eyes are open for either a Green Team truck or a seemingly abandoned truck with Trevor Simms's license plate number. That should be wrapped up by ten or eleven this morning."

"Great."

"What's even greater is that Deputy Director McGrath knows that you made that connection," Bryers said. "I made sure to tell him when I briefed him last night. I also let him know how delicate and efficient you were with Collette Simms. He's still not your biggest fan, but he seemed pleased."

"Is he a fan of anyone?" she asked, regretting the question as soon as it was out of her mouth. She certainly didn't want to seem as if she was bad-mouthing her superiors.

Bryers let out a chuckle and shrugged, dismissing the comment entirely. "Himself, maybe."

They drove on with the flow of early morning traffic as the tangle of Quantico/DC traffic started to thicken around them.

"Do we know where Lonnie Smith currently works?" Mackenzie asked.

"As a plumber's assistant," Bryers answered. "Before that, he was working in a warehouse and before that, in pulpwood mill. He's never held down a job for more than three years. I guess the brief prison stint probably didn't help at all, either."

"Any issues since getting out?"

"Nothing on file," Bryers said. "But as I'm sure you know, that rarely paints a full picture."

They arrived at Lonnie Smith's apartment complex twelve minutes later. It was a middle-of-the-road sort of place, not quite run down but certainly nowhere near respectable digs. Mackenzie followed Bryers up a single flight of stairs that wound through the interior of the building and then back out onto an almost motel-style walkway. They came to apartment 204, where Bryers stopped.

He didn't bother knocking on the door. There were two pieces of paper stuck to the door. They were both forms with letterhead that read BROOKVIEW APARTMENTS. The first form contained Lonnie's name, his apartment number, and then the number of the landlord. The brief form explained that Lonnie's rent was past due. The second form was identical to the first, only this one said that his rent was past due for a period of four weeks. The words FINAL NOTICE PRIOR TO EVICTION were scrawled at the bottom of the form in black marker.

"Want to call this number?" Bryers asked, pointing to the landlord's number.

Mackenzie nodded, pulling out her phone and punching the number in. The phone rang twice before it was answered by an irritable-sounding woman. She had a slight Asian accent and sounded very tired.

"Hello? This is Kim, with Brookview Apartments."

"Hi," Mackenzie said. "My name is Mackenzie White. I'm working as a consultant with the FBI on a local case that has led me to the apartment of one of your tenants."

"No surprise there," Kim said bitterly. "Who is it?"

"Lonnie Smith. My partner and I are standing outside his door right now and looking at the eviction notice."

"Well, if you find him, get the eleven hundred dollars he owes me, would you?"

Ignoring the woman's anger, Mackenzie said, "How long do you know for sure he's been gone?"

"I know he's been gone for at least six weeks," Kim said. "He's lived in that apartment for four years. His rent was always late—sometimes a day or two, sometimes two weeks. But then last month I went by to collect his late rent and he wasn't home. He hasn't answered calls and never comes to the door. I called the electric company and found that he had called and requested that his power be turned off six weeks ago."

"I understand," Mackenzie said. "Thank you for your time."

"Yes, fine. I hope you find the lowlife."

Mackenzie ended the call and headed back down the stairs with Bryers beside her. "Do you have the name and number of the plumber he was working for?" she asked.

"I do. I'll forward you the e-mail right now."

He sent the mail as they reached the car. By the time he was behind the wheel and pulling back out into the street, Mackenzie was on the phone with the owner of Pipeworks Plumbing. Again, she found herself enjoying how rapidly and fluidly information was exchanged within the Bureau. Compared to what she had known in Nebraska, it was almost like a magic trick.

When she had the manager of the plumbing company on the phone, she ran through introductions again, told the owner the same thing she had told Kim from Brookview Apartments, and got the same reaction.

"Yeah, I'm not too surprised the authorities are looking for him," the owner said.

"Why's that?" Mackenzie asked.

"He just always seemed shady. But I needed the help and when he showed up, he worked his ass off. But yeah…he called me about a month ago and said he was quitting. No reason, nothing. He sounded drunk when he called. It didn't surprise me…his work history was a joke and when I called his past employers, they told me not to expect him to stick around for long."

"Well, he is no longer living in his apartment," Mackenzie said. "Do you have any idea where he might have gone?"

"He gave me an address in South Carolina to send his final check to. That's all I have."

"Do you happen to have it?"

"Not on me right now."

"Could you e-mail it to me? I can give you my address."

They went through the formalities and within about ten minutes, she had the address to where the owner had sent Lonnie's last check. She filled Bryers in on everything the owner of

72

Pipeworks had told her, going over the details slowly so she could consider them all over again.

"Thoughts?" Bryers asked.

"I think this rules him out," Mackenzie said.

"You don't find his sudden disappearance *very* convenient?"

"It's noteworthy, certainly," she said. "But there are a few things to consider. First...this guy has commitment issues. Not just with work, but with a place of residence, apparently. It doesn't line up with the motivation and focus that it would take to kidnap someone, hold them captive for a while, kill them, and then dump them at a landfill after hours. We're talking about two different personality types. Also, someone like this would be on the lookout for their last paycheck before they landed their next job. The fact he had his last check delivered to South Carolina makes me think he's long gone—that he hasn't been anywhere near here for at least a month."

"All great points," Bryers said. "And I agree with all of it. Still, his disappearance in the wake of this, especially with even the slightest of links to Trevor Simms, makes him a priority. We need to call this in, give them all the available info, and let them churn their wheels. They'll try to find out where he's living, maybe even talk to some people involved in his attempted kidnapping from years ago. The good news for you and I is that we'll never touch any of that unless there's a proven link between Smith and these killings."

"I don't think there is," Mackenzie said.

"Same here."

"So now what do we do?" Mackenzie asked.

"We're at a standstill for now. Another dead lead. We get to anchor ourselves to the case files back at the office. What's your availability like today?"

"Well, it's Saturday. And I plan on making the most of the limited time I have. So I'll probably sit in my apartment and go over the files."

"You sound disappointed."

"It seems like a waste of time to just be sitting on my ass and trying to come up with something from the files," Mackenzie said. "Shouldn't we be out at the scenes, seeing if we overlooked anything?"

"Do you feel like you overlooked something?" Bryers asked.

"No."

"Exactly. There are other departments out there anyway, looking for stray traces like hair fibers and fingerprints. So far

73

there's been nothing. You and I are the lead on this...we have to be readily available. And sometimes that means sitting behind a desk and staring at photos and sheets of paper. Comes with the job, I'm afraid."

"How about the expiration clock I'm working against?"

"That usually *doesn't* come with the job," Bryers admitted. "And I'm going to try my hardest to make sure we beat that clock. I'll admit it: you've been thrown into a shitty situation. For them to potentially kick you out of the Academy for something you really didn't even have a hand in...that's messed up."

"Thanks," she said.

It was great to hear the support, but it did little good. She looked out her window as Saturday morning traffic trickled by and wondered if this might be her last weekend as a trainee.

And perhaps more importantly, she wondered where the killer was and what *his* plans for the weekend might be.

CHAPTER FOURTEEN

He kept thinking about the truck—that damned truck that he had somehow not even taken the time to think about when the lawn care man had come knocking. He'd let less than thirty seconds pass before he'd attacked the man. He'd then dragged his unconscious body back to his addition of the house to the soundtrack of his mother's blaring shows and her miserable coughing.

Once the lawn care man was safely stored away in the crawlspace, that's when the idea of a truck had occurred to him. The lawn care man had come here *somehow.* Probably in a company car because that was better for advertisement. He looked at the binder that had dropped from the man's hands in the brief skirmish and read the company name along the spine: The Green Team.

He went back into the crawlspace and found the man stirring. He punched him twice, hard in the head, knocking him out again. He then pulled him partially out of the crawlspace and patted him down for keys. He found them in the man's right front pants pocket. He then replaced the lawn care man, made sure the small door to his crawlspace was secured, and then walked back through his addition. When he was inside his mother's house, he told her he'd be gone for a while and then spent the next forty-five minutes walking around the neighborhood looking for a truck or van with the same The Green Team logo he had seen on the lawn care man's binder.

When he found it parked two streets over, he unlocked the door with the keys he'd taken from the lawn care man's pocket. He got inside quickly and started the engine. Before pulling off, he looked around the cab. There was no computer or tablet to be found, although there was a small planner. He opened it up to the day's date and saw where the lawn care man had marked down his planned stops for the day.

He tore the page out, balled it up, and shoved it into his pocket. He then pulled the truck away from the curb and headed east. He had no clear destination in mind; he simply wanted the truck as far away from his house as possible. He hated it when something unexpected happened, yet, at the same time, knew that problem-solving such a thing kept his mind sharp. And given the sort of hobbies he was into, keeping a sharp mind was very important.

He came to a stop half an hour away, parking the truck in an empty spot in a Burger King parking lot. He locked the doors, took the keys with him, and started walking. Already, he felt a huge weight lift from his shoulders. He walked five minutes to the closest bus stop and caught the next ride back home.

The whole ordeal had taken a little more than an hour and a half. He'd returned home to silence; the TV in his mother's room was off and even before he started down the hallway, he could hear her snoring. She'd nap until after two in the afternoon, leaving him to deal with the lawn care man that was trapped in his crawlspace.

That's how he spent the rest of that afternoon. He'd sat there, listening to the man's muffled pleas and screams. He knew his mother wouldn't hear the screams; he'd insulated the crawlspace for such sound back when he'd built it, pretty sure he'd be using it for this sort of thing in the future. It was a miserable little hole in the side of the addition, but it had served its purpose well. He hadn't had to buy anything too expensive—the simple insulation and an industrial-strength lock for the door was really all it took.

He listened to the man beg for his life for almost an hour. After a while, the muted noise was almost like the humming of an electric fan or the pleasant rattle of the air conditioning kicking on in the middle of the night. Soon, though, he tired of the sound and grew far too excited about what came next.

Slowly and methodically, like a man with an important job awaiting him, he retrieved his wooden baseball bat from beneath his bed. He then opened the door to the crawlspace, hunkered down inside, and quieted the man once and for all.

***

That had been two days ago. He knew this because of the nudie calendar on his bedroom wall. The woman for the month of September was a redhead with small breasts and incredible legs. He had placed a mark on Thursday (a small *) and had placed small dashes on the days that followed. That was the only way he could tell his days apart. Sometimes he forgot what day it was and what he had done the day before. But he knew that the mark on Friday meant that he had taken someone to the crawlspace, which meant that he had taken that same person to a landfill that night.

That meant today was Saturday. He looked to his cell phone and pulled his mother's calendar up. He had synced their calendars long ago, unbeknownst to her, so he would know when she had those stupid salespeople come over to peddle their useless crap. He saw that there was someone scheduled to come by today—someone from a company called Natural Health Remedies.

76

He Googled the company and found that it was a small business—owned and operated by a single woman that worked from home. Her website was cutesy and she made a big deal about how every facet of her business was run from her living room while she was trying to write the Great American Novel in her spare time. He knew that meant that there would be no co-workers or database of any kind that would know where she was headed later in the day. It made her the perfect candidate.

He deleted the entry from his mother's calendar and quickly walked into her part of the house. He made his way down the hallway, enveloped by the roar of whatever morning game show she was watching. He knocked on her door, heard her fumbling on the bed for the remote, and then the noise went quiet.

"Yeah?" she asked, her voice raspy and thick.

He cracked the door open, not even bothering to look inside. "I'm having a snack," he said. "You want something?"

He knew she would. She was going to want one of those God-awful pudding cups. Tapioca. She ate about four a day and there was constantly at least a case of the garbage in the pantry.

"Thanks, sweetie," she said. "Yeah, if you can bring me one of my puddings, that would be nice. And some juice, too."

"Sure thing."

He closed the door behind him and went into the kitchen. He popped open one of her tapioca pudding cups and poured her a cup of the orange pineapple juice she drank by the gallon. He then dug into his pocket and pulled out the three Sonata capsules he'd taken from his stash. He'd been prescribed the batch of Sonata last year when he'd been unable to sleep. He'd only taken four of them because he didn't like the groggy way he felt in the morning after taking them. He held on to them, though, knowing he'd need to use them on his mother one day.

He carefully separated the ends of the capsules and dumped the white powder into the pudding. He then swirled the pudding around, stirring it up to hide the powder. He waited a moment, not wanting to seem as if he had rushed things, and carried the snack to his mother. When he knocked this time, she did not bother turning down the television; she merely yelled for him to come in and then patted his hand lovingly when he set the pudding and juice down on her bedside table.

He managed not to look at her the entire time he was in the room. She was disgusting. Seeing what she had become made him feel ill. He remembered the slim, svelte mother he'd had as a boy and wondered what had happened to her. His father was partly to blame, but then again it wasn't his father who had shoved twenty-five years of unhealthy food into her mouth. His father had been a miserable excuse for a human being and had done lots of shitty things, but forcing his mother to gain more than two hundred pounds was not one of them.

He went back into his add-on and sat on the edge of his bed. He looked to the crawlspace that sat just outside of his room, installed in the wall like a strange trap-door. He then looked to his watch. It was 10:05. The appointment with the lady from Natural Health Remedies was at 11:30.

He could do nothing between now and then to ease the need that was even now consuming him from within.

All he could do was look at the entrance to the crawlspace and fantasize about what the next victim might be like. Would she scream? Would she beg for her life and offer sex? Or would she just melt into a blubbering mess?

He didn't care one way or the other. All he cared about was filling the hole—satisfying the need. The scary thing was that, for right now, he didn't see the need being fully satisfied anytime soon.

In the past, one victim had done it. He'd off one person and the itch would be scratched. One victim would last him several months. But now, ever since the woman named Shanda Elliot, the need had only grown stronger. And he had to satisfy it or the voices would start again…the voices that reminded him about his failure of a father and the things his father had done to him.

You liked it, didn't you? the voices would ask. *You liked it and when he walked out, that was the only thing you were sad about….that you wouldn't be his special little boy anymore.*

"Shut up," he said into the empty room. Even at the thought of those voices returning, he grew restless and borderline sick.

He had to keep the voices away. And he would do anything to do that…even if it meant more deaths to satisfy the hunger inside of him.

If it kept the voices away, he'd kill anyone and everyone. He'd kill *everyone*…burn down the whole world just for a moment's peace.

He looked to his watch. Eighty more minutes and she'd be here.

He could wait that long. The need could wait that long.

And if it couldn't…well, there was always his mother.

CHAPTER FIFTEEN

Mackenzie spent Saturday holed up in her apartment, looking over the case files. She spoke to Bryers only once in the time and that had merely been so he could update her on what was going on behind the scenes. A small team was still actively trying to locate Lonnie Smith but had come up with nothing so far. Also, they received information from the local PD that Trevor Simms's work truck had been discovered in a Burger King parking lot and towed away by the city. It was currently sitting in an impound lot and had been looked over by a forensics team that had found not a single trace of evidence. The only thing of note was that Thursday's log entries had been torn from Trevor's planner.

It was the planner that Mackenzie was thinking about Saturday afternoon as she sat at her small table in the kitchen, drinking a beer and listening to music. She stared at the contents of the files, the pictures of the landfills and victims, as if they were works of fine art to be admired and studied.

She wondered if Bryers would be able to get the planner for her. Having the page torn out indicated that the killer was logical. She also assumed that it had been the killer that had dumped the truck off in the Burger King parking lot, having moved what would have otherwise been a beacon for the FBI from his neighborhood.

She tried to envision herself as a murderer that was moving such a damning piece of evidence. To have left no evidence meant that he was not only careful, but also calm. It suggested that he felt no real remorse for what he did. He showed no panic, no laziness in his approach. And to show no remorse for his actions yet also have the logical aptitude to move the truck and take a page from a planner, it was also clear that he was *aware* of what he was doing. Dumping the bodies in landfills (state landfills at that) also indicated that he knew keeping the bodies for any period of time could also come back to harm him. Awareness of the murders without any remorse indicated some sort of psychological issue. If that were the case, there was a very good chance that their killer was killing with no real motive other than he enjoyed it.

Looking at the crime scene photos with this kindling of realization made her feel more worried than ever. A cold-blooded killer with intellect like that was going to be tricky to catch and, over time, a lot more brutal and routine in his actions.

Maybe, she thought as she finished her beer, *it will be the routine that leads us to him.*

As she continued to pore over the files, her phone rang. She dashed to it right away, thinking it would be Bryers. But the number on the display was unfamiliar. She answered it cautiously, wondering if Zack was using another number to get in touch with her, hoping to fool her. But the area code was DC, so that was probably not the case.

"Hello?"

"Hi, Mackenzie. How are you?"

"I'm…good. Who is this?"

"It's Colby Stinson."

"Oh…sorry. I didn't catch your voice and haven't saved your number to my phone yet."

"No worries. Look, I figured you for the type that would be stuck in your apartment on a Saturday night."

"That obvious?" she said, playing along so as not to reveal the fact that she was secretly helping with a case.

"Come on out and join me for a drink," Colby said.

"I don't know. I don't really feel like drinking." This, of course, was not true. But she'd just had a beer and wanted to remain alert and available in the event that Bryers called.

"Fine then," Colby said. "Come out and watch me have a drink."

Mackenzie looked down to the case files on the table. She knew them inside and out now, having spent the weekend poring over them. She wasn't going to extract anything new from them in the course of the next two hours or so. Besides that, some human interaction after the miserable twenty-four hours she'd had might do her some good.

"Sure, I can do that," Mackenzie said. "Where and when?"

They made plans and even as Mackenzie closed up the files, her mind remained on the contents inside of them. She went down a mental checklist in her head, trying to come up with a valid solution.

Most likely a male with some sort of psychological issues but is very clever. He is probably holding the victims in some sort of wooden cage or box that has insulation inside of it. No motive, just kills for the sport. So far, it seems all of the victims have come to him rather than him scouting them out.

The picture these facts painted was not pretty, but it at least gave her some color to work with. And it was that picture that remained in her head as she headed out the door in an attempt to resume a normal life.

She met Colby at a small diner two blocks away from the Academy. The place was mostly known for its thick, greasy burgers but Mackenzie had a soft spot for their omelets. She was enjoying one as she and Colby caught up. It was mostly small talk, some of which made Mackenzie a little envious. While Colby did not come out and say as much, she heavily eluded to a weekend fling with a guy from their Profiling class that kept them in bed most of Saturday.

Mackenzie tried to remember the last time she'd had sex. It had been over five months ago, a quick and rather unfulfilling session with Zack. She wondered then if she was going to end up being one of those women who was more interested in her career than men. However, given some of the impure thoughts she'd been having about Ellington as of late, she found that very hard to believe. She also knew that Harry would probably be more than willing, if she ever gave him the chance.

Maybe if my time runs out on this case and McGrath kicks me out, I'll run crying to Harry for consoling, she thought.

She listened to Colby as cordially as she could, nodding here and there and making comments at all the right points. But it wasn't until near the end of the meal that she *really* started listening. With the way Colby decided to wrap up their conversation, she had no choice but to pay close attention.

"So listen," Colby said. "I don't know how to say this to you, but I feel that I need to because I guess we're sort of friends, right?"

"Oh shit," Mackenzie said. "Is there another elephant?"

"Not quite an elephant this time."

"But some sort of large jungle creature?"

Colby shrugged, apparently done with the elephant business. "Well, just about everyone in our courses knows that you've been helping Agent Bryers on a case," she said. "Jealousy, of course, has reared its ugly head. Some of the things I've heard in the hallways is pretty bad."

"How bad?" Mackenzie asked, already feeling anger rise up inside of her. She didn't mind. She'd rather feel anger toward gossip than pity any day.

"Well, everyone thinks of you as this B-list celebrity anyway because of the Scarecrow Killer. So there's rumors of how you're all entitled and are just taking classes to go through the motions. There's also a rumor going around that you're sleeping with Bryers and that's how you got the job."

Mackenzie couldn't help but laugh. "Sleeping with Bryers? That's hilarious."

"Well, sleeping with *someone*. Mind you, I don't believe any of it."

"What do you believe?" Mackenzie asked.

Colby took a moment to think before verbalizing her answer. "I think the skill you showed in bringing in the Scarecrow Killer followed you here. And I also know that Bryers's old partner is now riding a desk somewhere. Not sure why. So Bryers needed a new partner and rather than promote from within, the powers that be decided it might be a good experiment to pair him with one of their most promising recruits."

"I like your theory much more," Mackenzie said.

Colby smiled. "Yeah, and it makes more sense. I'm all about sleeping with older men, but Bryers doesn't seem like the cradle-robbing type."

"Trust me, he's not."

"But…older men. Yay or nay?"

Mackenzie shook her head. "Not as old as Bryers. I have to draw the line somewhere."

It was good to get in some girl talk, even though it was tainted by the news that she was a point of nasty gossip among her peers. It did make her realize that she was isolating herself and becoming something of a hermit. When the only man she was spending time with was her partner, who was twenty-two years older than her, something had to give.

Maybe she'd work on that after this case was wrapped up. Because even as she and Colby joked about their sex lives, Mackenzie was still scrolling down the mental checklist in the back of her head, trying to nail down a profile on their killer.

CHAPTER SIXTEEN

He had almost an hour and a half to waste. He again thought of moving the Green Team truck and wondered if it had been towed yet. He almost hoped so. If the authorities were on to something yet, the random location of the truck would throw them off. They were much dumber than those glamorized shows on TV made them out to be.

Soon, 11:00 came, and then 11:15. He started to feel the familiar anxiousness in his gut, a feeling that radiated through him and was almost sexual in nature. At 11:20, he walked into his mother's house and tiptoed down the hallway. As he reached her door, he heard her sleeping, not quite snoring but with deep heavy breaths the doctors said would eventually lead her to needing a breathing device to help her sleep.

He walked back into the living room, sat on the couch, and thumbed through one of his mother's food magazines. He paid no attention to the words or pictures, thinking only of the woman that was on the way. He wondered what her pleas through the crawlspace would sound like. The lawn care man had been childlike and pathetic. Women, on the other hand, sometimes sounded almost sensual when they started crying for their freedom. Some had even offered to have sex with him, to do anything he wanted.

He'd never taken them up on it. While he loved the way women looked, especially the ones on his calendar and in the few old magazines his father had left behind in the attic all those years ago, the thought of sex was disgusting.

A knock at the door broke him out of his thoughts.

He set the magazine down and got up slowly, not wanting to seem too anxious. He took a deep breath and smiled as he approached the door, trying to make himself keep from trembling with anticipation. He composed himself and answered the door.

The woman on the other side was plain-looking, but could be pretty in the right light. She carried a canvas bag filled with books and samples. She smiled warmly at him and made a quick check over his shoulder, looking into the house.

"Hi," the woman said. "Is Mary home?"

"She is," he said. "Come on in and I'll get her for you."

"Thanks," the woman said, following him in. She thought he was harmless. Most women did. It was something about the way he looked; he wasn't threatening, nor was he good-looking. He was plain, he was average and easy to overlook. He'd known this since middle school and had always taken advantage of it.

When the woman was inside, he closed the door behind her and started for the hallway. When he was halfway there, he stopped and turned around to face the woman.

"You know, I think she's asleep right now."

"Oh. Should I come back later?"

"No, no not at all," he said. "Now's the perfect time."

"Oh, well I—"

He threw out his right hand quickly, punching her directly in the stomach. When she gasped out all of her breath and bent down, he grabbed her lovely brown hair, pulled back on it, and made her look at him. She opened her mouth to scream but something in her eyes seemed to flicker for a moment. Then, rather than scream, she brought her left arm up in a hard arc.

Her elbow caught him directly between the legs. The pain was immense and sickening. For a glaring moment, he thought of his father calling him his special boy, a memory associated with a similar pain.

The pain and the memory made him dizzy and he released the woman's hair. She got up quickly and instead of running, she delivered a hard kick to his stomach. The air went rushing out of him and as he fell to his hands and knees he saw that now the woman was choosing to run.

Her canvas bag had fallen to the floor, spilling out samples and stupid little books. He slapped at them with a hand as he let out a little howl of pain. Ahead of him, the woman had made it to the door and was unlocking it.

He pushed the pain aside, swallowing it down in a bitter pill that made him feel like he had to puke. He got to his feet and launched himself at the woman. He was actually airborne for about two seconds and as he sailed toward her, she had the door open. Saturday sunshine spilled in through the door.

His full weight collided with her lower legs. She toppled over, her head striking the doorway with a sickening thud. Her right arm fell outside, making a clawing gesture at the porch. He grabbed her by the shoulders and hauled her back inside, throwing her down to the floor. She was clearly a bit dazed from striking the doorway but was still getting to her feet.

She was standing on the porch, then stumbling down the concrete stairs.

His eyes went wide. Fear and anger spun into a cyclone within him and he was running after her before he could even think to stop himself. He dashed out of the door and launched himself from the porch just as she reached the bottom of the stairs.

He slammed into her back and they both went tumbling to the ground. He landed on top of her as she went skidding along the old cracked sidewalk that ran through his yard.

She was sobbing, clearly in pain, and trying to move. He drove an elbow into the small of her back and then slowly got to his feet. He looked around quickly, finding that he had been fortunate; no one was out on the streets. No one was walking their dog or passing by in their cars.

He again grabbed her by the hair, lifting her to her feet. She cried out weakly but then he placed his other hand around her throat. She sensed that she was not going to get out of this, and the fight went spiraling out of her. He nearly ran back into the house with her his hands still in her hair and at her neck. Inside, he slammed the door behind them and dropped her to the floor where she moved only the slightest bit. He then lowered himself down to her and ran a hand almost lovingly down the side of her face, then down her neck, then over her breasts, then her hips, then her knees.

With a smile, he hitched her up beneath the arms and started dragging her to the back of his mother's house, toward his addition. The crawlspace was empty again, and he could practically hear it calling out for someone to come occupy its dark spaces.

CHAPTER SEVENTEEN

When Mackenzie got to the landfill, it was just after eight o'clock in the morning. It was the landfill the first two victims had been found in and it was starting to look a little too familiar to her. She pulled her car in behind several others as she took in the commotion. There were a few state workers—landfill employees, no doubt—speaking with two agents. Beside them, she saw Bryers speaking on his cell phone. When he saw her, he beckoned her forward.

She got out of her car and walked quickly over to him. All she was able to hear of his conversation before he ended the call was a simple *"Yes sir. I'll see you then."*

He then gave Mackenzie his full attention and said: "That was fast."

"I was already on my way to the gym when you called."

"Well, I'm glad you're here," he said.

"Another body, you said?"

"That's right," Bryers said. "Another woman. She's still up there if you want to have a look."

She did, but did not want to seem too enthusiastic. She let Bryers lead her up the small hill to the dumpsters, directly toward the very same dump Susan Kellerman's body had been discovered in. Without a word shared between them, they came to the edge of the big green dumpster and looked in.

Mackenzie looked at the woman's body without blinking for about five seconds, just to make sure she was really seeing it. It was wasteful and it was sick, seeing a human body like this: lifeless and devoid of color, strewn in with candy wrappers, old coffee filters, dingy cardboard, and other refuse.

There was a scrape on the top of her forehead, mostly raw and not yet scabbed over. There was also a clear bruise just to the left of the center of her neck. She was completely naked and uncovered by the trash, lying on top of the pile.

"It gets worse," Bryers said.

"How so?" Mackenzie asked.

"McGrath is on his way. He's in full freakout mode. I almost called you back to tell you not to come, but I don't know how to play this."

"What do you mean?"

"He'll be irritated that you're here at all," Bryers explained. "But I thought it might be *worse* if you *weren't* here. He gave you forty-eight hours so I guess you should be present at something like this."

"Damned if I do, damned if I don't," Mackenzie said.

"Exactly."

"Another strike against us," Bryers said, pointing to the sky, "is the weather. Those gray clouds up there make me think we'll see rain within the hour."

"Has the medical examiner already come?"

"No. They're about ten minutes out. We just got the call an hour ago, from one of the workers down with the other agents. Everything is going a hundred miles a minute for this one. It quickly hit the top of the Bureau's priority list."

It took that last bit to clue Mackenzie in on just how high-profile this was becoming. And somehow, she had gotten stuck directly in the middle of it. Looking down to this dead woman—the fourth victim of what was now appearing to be a serial killer—she started to think that maybe McGrath was right. Maybe she had no business being involved in this.

"Our hands are tied until the ME gets here, right?" she asked.

"Yeah."

"Maybe we can find something down by the chain-link fence again?" she suggested.

"You can try. But remember how well that worked out last time."

There was a hint of annoyance in his voice that Mackenzie decided to ignore. As her partner (technically), the whole situation was just as messy for him. She understood it, but she didn't have time to sympathize.

She headed back down to the bottom of the small hill to where the chain-link fence separated the dump from the feeder road. She had made it halfway down when a car came speeding up the feeder road. It came to a jarring stop just inches behind Mackenzie's car. She watched as McGrath got out, wasting no time as he sauntered through the gate and straight toward her.

When he stopped several inches away from her, he did not look angry per se. He looked like a man with a hell of a lot of pressure and weight on his shoulders and she just happened to be in the way.

"Mrs. White," he said, remaining as calm as he could, "because of this death, things are getting out of hand with this case. There's no apparent time-table for this killer and within a few hours, an ungodly amount of Bureau resources are going to be poured into this. And the more people that get involved, the harder it's going to be to stay hush-hush about your involvement."

"I see," Mackenzie said. She felt anger and disappointment trying to flare up but she did understand where he was coming from. After all, this was not about her...this was about tracking down a killer. She was a bit ashamed that she was letting her ambition cloud her priorities.

"However," McGrath said, "I am a man of my word. I gave you forty-eight hours. And by my estimation, you still have twenty-two. But I can't have you here, in the middle of all of the commotion. I'm going to have to stick you with family duty."

"But sir, I can be a valuable asset here and—"

"This is non-negotiable," he said. "I expect you off of this scene within two minutes. I don't care where you go, just don't stay here. I'll see to it that Agent Bryers gets you the contact information for the family the moment we make a positive ID. That's the only favor you'll get from me."

Mackenzie knew that she *had* to do as he said. Not only was he extending an olive branch by keeping her on the case at all given the recently escalated nature of the case, but she also needed to stay in the good graces of everyone that that sticking their necks out for her, making sure she was still involved.

"Yes, sir," she said. She gave a curt little nod and headed back for the gate and her car beyond. She didn't look back toward the dumps until she reached her car and opened the door. She found Bryers's face among the growing crowd. He was staring in her direction and she was touched to see that he looked sad and disappointed.

She gave a small wave as she stepped into the car. Then she started the ignition and backed out. Before she reached the end of the feeder road and was back on the main highway, the first small droplets of rain fell and started to patter against her windshield.

***

She certainly wasn't going to head back to her apartment, and she didn't want to go to the gym to start a workout that she would get interrupted from. Being a Sunday, retreating to the Academy or the firing range was also out of the question. She felt strange—not dissatisfied but somehow depressed all at the same time.

She decided to hit up a Starbucks, where she ordered a dark brew and simply sat in the back of the shop, scrolling through her phone and listening to the light drizzle of rain tap against the window. As she looked through her contacts, she started to understand the feeling that was sweeping through her. She hated to admit it—hated to lower herself to what felt like the emotional state of a teenager—but she was lonely.

Her finger hovered over Harry's name for a few moments before she decided to press it. She then held the phone to her ear and listened, trying to remember the last time she had called a man she wasn't working with.

Harry answered on the second ring. He sounded like he was tired, but trying to hide it.

"Hello?" he asked.

"Harry…it's Mackenzie."

"Yes, my magical cell display told me so."

"What are you up to?"

"Not much," he said. There was an edge of curiosity to his voice. Clearly, he was trying to figure out why she had called. "I thought you'd be fast on the heels of a killer by now."

"What?"

Harry hesitated for a moment before coming clean. "Everyone knows you were tapped to help on a case."

"Does everyone know which case?"

"I don't know," he said. "I know that *I* don't. So…is it true?"

"I can neither confirm nor deny," Mackenzie said.

"What if I get you liquored up? Would you talk then?"

"It depends on what we're drinking and how much we're drinking," she said. "But in all honesty…it's all too much right now."

"What is?" Harry asked.

"Nothing I can talk about, really."

"Oh. Well if you can't talk about it, why did you call?"

"I don't know."

"I mean, I'm glad you did," Harry said.

Silence filled the line and the awkwardness that fell between them reminded Mackenzie of why she had never bothered calling boys. Even from as early as her teenage years, she'd hated it.

"What are you doing later today?" Mackenzie asked. The question came out suddenly, almost like a burp it was so unexpected.

"*When* today?" he asked.

"Later. Like in the afternoon."

"Nothing much. How about you?"

"I don't know yet. But if I happen to be free, I thought we could maybe get those drinks."

"So, you want me to be available in the off chance that *you're* available," Harry said. "Is that about right?"

"That sums it up, yes," she said with a laugh. Hearing her own laugh was odd. She didn't really care for it.

"I think I can do that," Harry said.

"Good. I'll call you."

"If you're free," Harry pointed out.

"Yes. If I'm free. Bye, Harry."

"Bye," he said, with that edge of curiosity still in his voice.

She felt slightly empowered to have survived the call and was pleasantly surprised that she hoped things worked out and they *could* get together in the afternoon. While her feelings for Harry were nowhere near what his seemed to be for her, she wondered if it would be *so* bad to kiss him...to have his hands on her and to feel *wanted*. While she had obviously been intimate with Zack numerous times just before their breakup, he had not made her feel wanted in a very long time.

Feeling as if the phone call had given her some sort of courage she'd not had in quite some time, Mackenzie scrolled further down into her contacts. She stopped at *MOM*.

Again, her finger hovered. She hadn't spoken to her mother since moving to Quantico. And while she doubted her mother even cared, there was a sense of responsibility that had been evolving into guilt over the last few weeks. While things with her mother and sister were strained, there was no reason to completely cut them off.

She nearly pressed *MOM* but the phone buzzed in her hand as she lowered her thumb. The display screen now showed *BRYERS*.

She answered quickly, feeling a little derailed from taking a moment to sort through her own personal matters. "Hey, Bryers."

"Hey," he said. "Look...sorry about how things worked out. McGrath is right, though. This thing is about to become a circus."

"I know. It's fine."

"Sure. The tone of your voice says otherwise."

"Did they get a positive ID already?" she asked.

"Yeah. And I'm going to text you over an address. The victim was Dana Moore, thirty-one, single. The only person we've contacted so far is her mother. Seems to be the only family she had."

"Okay. Thanks."

"You okay?" Bryers asked. She recalled the disappointed look she'd seen on his face when she'd left the landfill. His genuine concern meant a lot to her and, truthfully, it *did* make things a little closer to okay.

"Yeah," she said. "I'll keep you posted if I find anything from the mother."

"I look forward to it," Bryers said.

Mackenzie ended the call and took her coffee with her as she headed out the door. The rain was still coming down in a sprinkle, hesitant drops falling just frequently enough to be annoying. She heard her phone chime as Bryers sent her the address and she wasted no time in pulling it up.

She had twenty hours remaining and she was going to make every single one of them count. More than that, she was going to do a good job, regardless of what bullshit detail McGrath stuck her with. With the rain still falling, Mackenzie got back behind the wheel of her car and went to speak to the third mourning family member in the last two days.

CHAPTER EIGHTEEN

Gloria Moore was in a state of shock when Mackenzie got there. Mackenzie felt bad for the fifty-five-year-old woman but would much rather deal with utter shock and disbelief than outright sorrow and wailing. She'd only received the call confirming her daughter's death forty minutes ago and if Mackenzie had to guess, the full weight of the news had not yet registered. Right now, she simply looked tired and terribly confused.

She'd invited Mackenzie in right away, but walked through the house like a zombie. They'd settled down in a Gloria's small living room and had sat in silence for a good twenty seconds before Mackenzie understood that it was going to take some prodding to get Gloria Moore out of her stupor.

"I know it may be hard to sort through these sorts of things right now," Mackenzie said, "but any information you can give me right now could potentially help us find the man who did this."

"Yes, I know," Gloria said. Her voice was robotic and monotone.

"Do you know if Dana had any enemies? People that she simply didn't get along with?"

"None that I can think of," Gloria said. "She was a very quiet girl. She kept to herself."

Mackenzie wondered about the family dynamic at play in the Moore household. Gloria lived on her own and Mackenzie had seen no family pictures—no sign of a father figure. Perhaps Gloria had raised Dana to also be something of a loner.

"Had there been any significant developments in her life lately?" Mackenzie asked "Anything that might have had her spending time with new people?"

Gloria took a moment to think about it and then started to slowly nod. "Well, she'd finally started to gain some traction with her job. She works from home and had just barely been getting by. But about two months ago, things starting ramping up—something about Facebook promotions."

"What sort of work was it?"

"She sold diet pills and vitamin supplements. She called her business Natural Health Remedies."

"Any co-workers?"

"No. It was just her. It was a door-to-door job, really. She had people call to set up appointments. Sometimes they met at coffee shops and sometimes she made house calls. Not very exciting…but she was happy to have it."

Something in Mackenzie's mind clicked—almost as smooth as a key slipping into a lock. *Door to door.* While Trevor Simms had not worked a door-to-door job, he *had* been going door to door in an effort to drum up business during the time he died. And what about Susan Kellerman? Hadn't there been something said about her job that might at least indicate that she had been going door to door? She'd have to go back through the notes, but she thought there might be a link there.

Suddenly, the door-to-door theory she and Bryers had discussed seemed like much more than a theory.

"Would you allow me to have access to her computer?"

"That's fine," Gloria said, "but I couldn't even start to tell you what her passwords are. But if you want, I think I have a few names of her clients. She was always trying to get me to use the stuff she was selling. She always told me the success stories and invited me to call some of her clients."

"That would be terrific."

"One second," Gloria said.

As the woman got to her feet, she swayed a bit. Mackenzie could practically see the grief catching up with her. Mackenzie wasn't sure how much longer she would last before she broke. According to Bryers, the next of kin, Gloria's sister, should be arriving shortly. It made Mackenzie feel a little guilty, but she hoped she was long gone before any sort of comfort or sympathy would need to be extended.

Less than a minute later, Gloria came back with two Post-it notes. There were three names on one and two on the other. Each name had a phone number beneath it. One of them was circled and Gloria pointed to the circled name as she handed the Post-its over. The name that was circled was Becka Rudolph.

"This one," Gloria said, "is Dana's most loyal client. I think she got at least two orders a month."

Mackenzie took the names and pocketed them, anxious to follow up on them before McGrath thought to check up. As if the gods were continuing to smile on her even after McGrath's instructions at the landfill, a knock on Gloria's door gave her the permission to leave that she needed. Even if she *was* a bit emotionally unstable, she still wasn't about to leave a grieving mother alone so soon after having lost her daughter.

Still walking in that zombie-like state, Gloria walked to the door. When she answered it and saw the other woman on the other side—the appearance too uncanny to *not* be her sister—Gloria seemed to collapse inward. She folded and then went to her knees, wailing. The woman at the door gave Mackenzie a nearly apologetic look and then went to her sister, also dropping to her knees to embrace Gloria.

Mackenzie could only stand there awkwardly for a moment. While in the presence of these women's sorrow, a very familiar anger and determination stirred inside of Mackenzie. She'd felt it for the first time when she had crossed some sort of mental line when hunting down the Scarecrow Killer and now here it was again. It was almost overwhelming, both motivating and painful inside.

It felt like someone had kicked up a nest of hornets in her guts. Mad and angry, those hornets had come out of hiding and were swarming.

***

Mackenzie called Becka Rudolph before she even pulled out of Gloria's driveway. Becka had just been getting out of church and had seemed genuinely saddened by the news of Dana Moore's death.

Half an hour later, Mackenzie found herself parking in a coffee shop lot to meet with her.

Becka was roughly Gloria's age—maybe slightly younger—and looked extremely uncomfortable when Mackenzie sat down with her. She was sipping from a coffee, still dressed in a slightly above-casual outfit.

"How well did you know Dana outside of your professional relationship?" Mackenzie asked.

"Fairly well, I guess. She was always personable, you know? She'd come to the house and drop off my order and then show me some of the new things coming up. But after that, she always took the time to ask me how things were going. I wouldn't say we were friends, but we were certainly on a friendly basis, I suppose."

"How long had you been her client?" Mackenzie asked.

"About three months. She always told me that I was just the second order she'd ever received. And I don't think he'd been doing business for much more than those three months."

"Would you happen to know how she kept up with her clientele? Did she have a calendar or anything?"

"She kept all of that on her iPhone," she said. "Whenever she set me up for a new order, she added it to the calendar on her phone."

"And when were you due for another order?"

"Two weeks from now," Becka said.

"I know this is a long shot, but by any chance do you know any of her other clients? Maybe you have some sort of idea of where she visited in the last few days?"

"No, I'm sorry. I don't. I would—"

"What is it?"

Becka took a moment to think, visibly making an effort to recover a memory.

"Wait…actually, I remember her saying that she was excited about a new potential client. It was a woman that has been in really bad health—an overweight lady. Dana said it was in a part of town she usually didn't travel to. She thought it was a great opportunity to drum up more business."

"Do you know what area that might be?" Mackenzie asked.

"All I know is that it was somewhere on the west side of town. Black Hill Street, maybe?"

"Do you mean Black *Mill* Street?" Mackenzie asked.

"Yes. I'm almost positive."

The sensation Mackenzie had felt of a key slipping into a lock became a turning of that key as yet another connection was made. Suddenly, she was furious that Bryers had not taken her seriously enough to follow up on the Black Mill Street lead they'd had earlier. She understood why he hadn't, but still…

She prepared to get up and leave.

"Wait," Becka said. "That seems sort of…cold. There's nothing else you need to know?"

Confused, Mackenzie did her best to think of any other questions that might appease the woman. She was on a clock here and wanted to get moving; she didn't have time to coddle a woman to make her feel important just because she was helping with the investigation.

"No ma'am. As I said, we're sort of on the clock here and—"

"Let me see some identification," Becka said, suddenly stern and defensive.

Mackenzie had left the plastic card on the lanyard in her car. Admitting that would seem incredibly novice of her but given the circumstances, she had no choice. *Idiot,* she thought to herself.

"I don't have any," she said. "I'm on a temporary consultant basis with the Bureau. I'm still in the Academy and was asked to—"

"I'm done here then," Becka said, suddenly standing to her feet. She looked furious and betrayed.

"It's okay," Mackenzie said, managing to keep her calm. "Really, I've been authorized to work this case."

"Even if that's the case, I don't appreciate your cold and businesslike approach to the death of what was a sweet woman. Now if you'll excuse me."

Mackenzie watched Becka Rudolph storm angrily out of the coffee shop and then uttered a shaky: *"Shit."*

Still, the Black Mill Street connection was suddenly very promising. Susan Kellerman had been headed there before she died and now there was a link to Dana Moore as well. Finding an address for someone that was in poor health might be harder, and she'd need bureau resources to do it. Surely McGrath would allow her to run with it.

And if he didn't?

She couldn't wait to find out.

Feeling a new sense of urgency course through her, Mackenzie went back out to her car and pulled up GPS directions for Black Mill Street.

CHAPTER NINETEEN

With what she felt was a solid lead in place, Mackenzie weighed her options. She could sit on it and wait to continue pursuing it herself—which was what she wanted to do—and possibly get McGrath even more pissed at her. Or she could notify Bryers right now and hope that McGrath and everyone working beneath him would have the good sense to follow up on it.

She decided that given the tumultuous nature of her current situation, the best thing to do would be to call Bryers. She did so. But when she revealed what she had discovered in conversations with Gloria Moore and Becka Rudolph, he was not nearly as pleased as she had anticipated.

"Look, Mackenzie," he said. "I'm going to be as honest and straight with you as I can, okay?" Bryers said.

"Okay."

"If McGrath told you to speak to the family, that's *all* he meant. Questioning someone not directly involved with the victim was outside of the permissions he gave you. If there's even the slightest hiccup with this Becka Rudolph lady, it could all be very bad for you."

"Fine, I get it," Mackenzie said. "I went too far. I'll stop. But can you please pass the Black Mill Street information on? It *can't* be a coincidence, can it?"

Bryers sighed through the phone and it was nearly deafening. "Look, I'll pass this on to McGrath, but if he asks how you got the information, I have to tell him the truth. You could get your wrist slapped for reaching out to Becka Rudolph."

"That's fine. Just…what else can I do?"

"For right now, I'd just wait. I'm the go-between right now, the middleman for you and McGrath. Of course, he just wants you completely off of this and—"

Mackenzie's phone beeped, signaling that she had an incoming call. She checked the display and did not recognize the number. "Bryers, can I get back to you? I've got another call."

"Sure. Bye for now."

Mackenzie switched over to the incoming call. "This is Mackenzie White," she said.

"White," a man's voice said. "Just what in the almighty hell do you think you're doing?"

The voice was filled with fury, making it easy to figure out who it was. McGrath was on the other end and he was beyond pissed.

"Doing what you asked, sir. I spoke with the mother."

"And then what?"

"She gave me a promising lead that I followed up with."

"I know that. A woman named Dana Moore. You know *how* I know? Because she called the FBI mainline and lodged a formal complaint against you. No badge and she said you were very rude. Imagine how I felt getting a phone call like that from the main office."

"I wasn't rude. I was just to the point and—"

"I don't care *what* you were. You had no right to speak to her at all! You weren't authorized."

"I'm sorry, sir. But I had to follow up on—"

"No. Those nineteen or twenty hours you had remaining are revoked. You're now officially off this case. I'll have a talk with the director to see if I can convince him to let you stay in the Academy."

"But there's a lead. A very promising lead, and it can—"

"Quiet, White," he snapped. "You're done with this case and I hope to not speak to you again until you've graduated the Academy. Am I understood?"

Fuming and furious, Mackenzie had to bite her lip to not retaliate. Finally, through clenched teeth, she nearly hissed: "Yes, sir."

"Good."

Without a goodbye or anything similar, McGrath ended the call. Mackenzie could feel herself trembling with anger as she threw her phone hard across the car in frustration. She slammed a hand against her steering wheel and let out a barking curse, realizing that she was extremely close to having a mental breakdown on the freeway.

She took several deep breaths to calm herself and, although she hated to feel as if she was retreating, she headed to her apartment. She could not ever remember feeling so defeated and alone. Even after discovering the body of her father, dead on the bed all those years ago, she'd had the police that had shown up to the scene and her catatonic mother to lazily console her. But now she was alone, in a city she barely knew, knowing there was a killer on the loose that she had failed to catch.

And maybe she never would.

CHAPTER TWENTY

Mackenzie went back to her apartment and knew she should let it go. But she could not. Rather than mope around, she again went to the case files. She had never been one to give in to defeat. And she wasn't about to start now.

Mackenzie knew that she had pored over them and had missed nothing, but it was the only productive thing she could think to do. Maybe if the case files presented something to her, she could at least run it by Bryers—if McGrath hadn't already ordered him to stay away from her.

Just as she was slipping the files back into the folders, her cell phone rang. Her heart leapt in her chest, as she was sure it would be Bryers or McGrath, telling her that something new had come up and they had decided they needed her after all. It was a childish hope, but one she could not deny.

When she saw Zack's number, the soaring feeling in her heart turned to a weight and she got irrationally mad. Any other time, she might have simply ignored the call and let him speak to her voicemail again. But she was mad, tired, and somewhere between frustrated and livid…and she needed to relieve it somehow.

She answered the phone on the third ring and didn't even pretend to be nice. "What is it now, Zack?" she asked.

The tone of her voice must have surprised him; he hesitated a moment before responding. "Well, it's nice to hear your voice, too," Zack said. He was trying to sound hurt but had the tone of someone that was looking to start a fight.

"You called me," Mackenzie pointed out. "What do you want?"

"I wanted to make sure you were still happy there."

"I am," she said, realizing just how big of a lie it was in that moment.

"So I'm supposed to believe that you don't miss me at all?"

"Believe it," she said. "I have a clean apartment without anyone to clean up after once I've come home for the day."

"Why do you have to be so damn mean about it?" he asked.

"Because sometimes I think that's the only way to get through to you."

Again, he hesitated. She could sense a change in the silence now, as if he was maybe formatting another method of attack.

"Was it really that bad?" he asked, suddenly sounding like a victim.

She bit back the first response that jumped to her tongue and this time it was her that hesitated. "It wasn't at first," she said. "But honestly, none of that matters now. None of it. I'm gone, Zack. It's over. It didn't work."

"I just wanted to make sure you still felt that way," he said. "Because as of now—after this conversation is over—I'm giving up. I want you back...well, I think I do, but you're making it clear how you feel. I'm done now, too. So when things don't work out for you up there, you can forget about me. I won't be here waiting for you when everything falls out from under you."

A slight wave of relief swept through her but given the way her day had gone, a retreat back to Nebraska suddenly didn't seem like such an impossible outcome.

"Good to know," was all she said, though. "Look, Zack, I'm sorry but I have to go."

"Ah, the busy bee," he said mockingly. "I almost forgot. Go on, Mac. Get out there and catch those bad guys."

The comment stung and she was unable to remain civil. "Fuck you," she said, and then ended the call.

She clenched her fists and then unclenched them, nearly throwing her phone for the second time that afternoon. She took a series of deep breaths, trying to calm herself. Nothing seemed to work.

Then, acting on impulse only, she simply remained tense and angry as she thumbed through the contacts on her cell phone and called Harry.

He answered quickly and when he did, Mackenzie was brief and to the point.

"You still available for those drinks tonight?" she asked.

***

Thirty minutes later, she was in the shower. The hot water slowly started to soothe her, and as she came down from the anger and frustration, she very seriously considered calling Harry to cancel the night's plans. The only reason she decided not to in the end was because she had taken a huge step in even calling him earlier that day. She was making progress in all areas of her life and while her social life didn't seem particularly important right now, it was still a form of growth. She wouldn't let a venomous conversation with Zack change that.

Forty-five minutes later, she was dressed and ready to head out. Before she walked out the door, she checked her e-mail with her phone one last time. Naively, she was still hoping someone within the chain of command would realize what an asset she could be and invite her back on the case.

She got no such confirmation when she looked to her phone. Other than a few junk e-mails, there was nothing new to see. With a scowl that quite honestly made her feel like a pouting child, she left her apartment, determined to allow herself not to care as the night progressed. She'd been given an amazing opportunity and it was her own damned fault that it had not worked out. She had no one to blame but herself and for now, she was perfectly fine with placing the blame where it needed to fall.

She walked to the bar they'd agreed upon, as she didn't want to go through the awkwardness of having Harry drive her home if she had too much to drink. It was just a four-block walk and she took that time to try to slip back into the dating mindset. The last guy she'd seriously dated had been Zack and the courting aspect of their relationship had not lasted very long at all. They'd been living together five months after they met—a decision Mackenzie looked back on with deep regret. She wondered if she still even *knew* how to date. She'd never been great at conversations with men, much less flirting…not that she needed to flirt with Harry. She knew that he was into her and that made tonight's date at least a little less intimidating.

When she arrived, it was just after six and he was already sitting at a small back booth with a beer in front of him. When he saw her meandering through the small crowd toward him, he flashed her a shy smile.

"You're early," Mackenzie said as she sat down across from him.

"I am," Harry said. "What can I say? I was excited."

"So how are you, Harry?" Mackenzie asked.

He looked perplexed at the question but the smile remained on his face. "Me? I'm good," he said. "This last half of the Academy is sort of trickling by—going way too slow, you know? But I'm enjoying it. Not as much as you, apparently. How goes the case? Or…can you not tell me?"

She shrugged and nearly started telling him everything that had happened in the course of that day. But rather than bring his mood down, she figured it was wisest to keep it vague. "It's a learning process for sure," she said. "High and lows all coming at me within the space of just a few days."

"Were you not ready for it?" Harry asked.

"I don't know," she said.

"I thought the Scarecrow Killer thing would have been a pretty good learning experience."

She rolled her eyes. "It was. But I'm starting to learn that one stupid case is quickly starting to define me."

"Oh," he said, clearly embarrassed.

"No, it's okay. I guess most normal people would be thrilled to get that kind of attention."

"You're not normal?"

"Far from it."

They shared an awkward laugh as the waitress came by to take their drink orders. Mackenzie took that time to give Harry a quick once-over. He was good-looking but in a very subtle way. But she already knew this from spending so much time with him at the Academy. She was pretty sure he had been the toddler that had been the cutest in his pre-school class, only to grow into an awkward teen that wouldn't develop the least bit of sex appeal until midway through college. Thinking of sex appeal and Harry within the same thought was a little weird and it was then and there that Mackenzie was relatively sure that there would be no romance blossoming between them. She hoped he felt it too, so she wouldn't have to be the one to spell it out.

The conversation between them was pleasant enough. She learned that Harry had grown up in Michigan and had turned down a baseball scholarship at MSU to pursue his dream of being an FBI agent. His parents had moved to California when he'd graduated high school and he had a dog. In turn, Mackenzie didn't offer much about herself. She kept information about her childhood to a minimum, refusing to venture anywhere near what it had been like to grow up with a father that had died suspiciously. Vaguely, she wondered if she was being as vague as Bryers had been to her and, if so, how it made Harry feel.

She did respect Harry quite a bit for not badgering her with questions about the Scarecrow Killer or her very brief stint in helping Bryers. It made her think that he was genuinely interested in her and maybe even as smitten as Colby joked about. He certainly looked at her in a way that indicated that he had more in mind than just a friendship.

"So what happens with you after the Academy?" Harry asked her.

"I'd like to go into Profiling," she said.

"Ah, so you must *love* McClarren's class."

"I do. I have my last session in that class tomorrow, as a matter of fact."

"So does it feel real to you yet?"

"Does *what* feel real?"

"The fact that we're almost there....almost done with the Academy part to all of this."

It actually *did* seem real to Mackenzie, mostly because of how she had spent the last two days. She was still tired and upset about how McGrath had dismissed her earlier in the day, so it was very hard to separate her Academy life from what she had caught a glimpse of over those two days. Still, she didn't want to move Harry into that discussion.

"Not really," she lied. "But I'm getting there."

Silence fell across the table and she did her best to return Harry's gaze without seeming too uncomfortable. There were three empty glasses in front of her—the third having just been emptied of its contents of a rum and Coke. She was feeling buzzed but not anywhere close to drunk. And that was good...if she had anything else to drink, there was no telling what she might end up telling Harry.

"Another?" he asked.

"No, sorry," she said. "Three is my limit. Actually, it's usually two. I made a special exception for you."

"Really?"

"Yeah. I gave you short notice and you still came."

"Of course I did. Are you okay to drive?"

"I walked," she said.

"Well, can we pay up and I'll walk you home?"

She spent a few seconds trying to think of a polite way to decline the gesture but could come up with nothing. She gave him a half-hearted smile and nodded. "That sounds fine," she said.

After a bit of friendly bickering, Harry convinced her to let him pay for her drinks. She only gave up when he demanded that he would likely one day owe it to her because based on the way training with her in Hogan's Alley was going, he'd one day owe her his life. So drinks as a mortgage on the future was a decent trade, he joked.

Outside, night had fallen and the city was mostly quiet. The air was just a few degrees away from being chilly and the slight buzz was making Mackenzie feel pleasant. It did not, however, make her unobservant. She noticed right away that Harry was walking incredibly close to her; every few steps, their arms would brush each other.

"You asked me earlier how I was doing," Harry said. "But let's be real here....how are *you*? And please don't bullshit me. You can trust me. I'm not going to spread any rumors or gossip."

She was so surprised by his bluntness that she nearly stopped walking and turned to look at him. But she wanted the walk home to be as quick and painless as possible. She was already pretty sure she was going to have to explain to him that she didn't want anything more than a friendship with him. So she kept walking, having already covered two blocks. Then, given the stern approach of the question, she rewarded him with the most honesty she'd shown him all night.

"I'm confused and a little out of my depth," she admitted. "The things we're picking up in the Academy certain apply to everything I've seen over the last few days but...I don't know. There's nothing to really prepare you for how it's all handled."

"How do you mean?"

"It's all very machinelike. Sure, finding a solution is at the end of the process but everything before that is more rigid than I was expecting. Of course, that might be because I'm not even supposed to be on the damn case anyway."

She sensed that she had said too much, the words propelled by a tongue loosened by liquor. But still, it felt good to get even that little bit of frustration out.

"Do you regret it?" he asked.

"No," she said right away, surprising even herself with the answer.

"Well, I guess that's the important thing."

They fell into silence as they crossed the last block. Harry still walked extremely close to her, making her feel both comforted and claustrophobic all at once. When her apartment came into view, Mackenzie stopped and nodded ahead.

"This is me," she said.

Harry looked to the building with mild interest. He looked nervous and a little uncertain. As Mackenzie walked the rest of the way to the door, Harry followed—now with a little distance between them.

"Thanks for calling me and asking me out," Harry said, almost as shy as a grade school boy.

"I thought it was time we saw each other outside of simulated real-life scenarios where our lives fictionally hang in the balance," she joked, trying to keep it light.

"You think we could do it again?" Harry asked.

The question hung in the air in a way that Mackenzie felt like she could maybe reach out and flick it. "Maybe," she said.

No sooner had the answer come out of her mouth than Harry was leaning forward. His eyes were closing and his hand was suddenly on her hip. She froze for a moment, not sure how to prevent the kiss from happening without seeming hostile. But it was suddenly too late. His lips were on hers and his hand was drawing her forward.

Call it instinct or the simple need to feel connected to someone, but Mackenzie allowed it to happen. She even placed her hand on his shoulder and pulled him closer to her, adding a sense of urgency to the kiss. His lips were firm and his hand on her hip was soft but eager. He was hesitant, a true gentlemen, she supposed, so it was she who extended things by parting her lips and touching his tongue with her own.

She wasn't sure how long the kiss lasted but all she knew was that whether she was attracted to him or not, she could not let things continue out of the impulse of inviting him to her apartment. The kiss was a good one despite the lack of a strong attraction and she feared her unrealized terror of being alone would prompt her to much more than just a kiss.

So finally, she broke the kiss and took a step back. "Good night," she said abruptly.

"Was that…are you okay?" Harry asked.

"I'm fine. It's just…I need to head up. I'll call you sometime later, though."

"Okay," Harry said, clearly wanting to ask more questions or extend the conversation.

Mackenzie didn't allow that to happen, though. She turned for the door, not looking back to Harry a single time. She did not slow her pace until she was inside the building and heading up the stairs to her apartment.

What the hell was that?

It was a good question. Why had she even allowed Harry to kiss her? Beyond that, why had she given in so easily and let him buy the drinks?

Was she *that* desperate for company? Was she *that* in need of some sort of acceptance after getting the boot from McGrath?

She slowly walked back to her apartment, feeling like she was unsure of everything. She'd failed at the task set before her by Bryers and Ellington (albeit an impossible task) and now had apparently forgotten how to interact with men that were attracted to her.

Worse than all of that, a very distant part of her brain could hear the ghosts of Nebraska calling her back home, luring her with the moans and cries of moments that had not only defined her past, but seemed to be ruining her future as well.

CHAPTER TWENTY ONE

A restless night's sleep had Mackenzie trudging into McClarren's course the following morning with puffy eyes and a cheerless disposition. She'd downed three cups of coffee so far but all that seemed to do was make her stomach upset. Any more caffeine anytime soon and she'd have the jitters. So she did her best to pay attention, a bit saddened that she wasn't able to fully absorb the lecture.

As she took notes, she wondered what sorts of things someone like McClarren had endured in the course of his career. She watched him idly as she jotted down her notes, wondering how someone who had seen so much in his career could seem so normal and logical. Sure, his age showed (he was only sixty-six but looked closer to eighty) but the man was brilliant and, at the same time, seemed no different than anyone else.

She'd only gotten the briefest taste of what it was like to delve into the darker parts of the human psyche while chasing down the Scarecrow Killer and that alone had been a bit too close to touching the darkness than she would ever care to get. McClarren, on the other hand, had been there many times—had, in fact, studied, analyzed, and tried his best to sympathize with and understand some of the most hardened murderers in American history. And yet here he was standing in front of a classroom, earning a paycheck and paying taxes just like anyone else.

She spent most of the class in this analytical daze, so enthralled and burdened by it that she was genuinely surprised when McClarren called the time and dismissed them. Mackenzie even checked her watch to see if he had dismissed them early but saw that it was indeed eleven o'clock, the usual ending time for the class.

She gathered up her things slowly, hating to admit that the best thing for her would not be her usual trip to the firing range or the gym, but back to her apartment to sleep. But as she headed for the doors, she heard her name spoken loudly over the slight commotion of Academy students filing out.

"Ms. White?"

She stopped and turned back toward the class. Down on the lecture floor, McClarren was looking directly at her.

She took a few steps back into the room and said, "Yes, sir?"

"Could you stick around for a bit?" he asked.

"Sure," she said, walking down to the floor where he still stood by his lectern. He had no desk, just a simple little podium which he rarely stood behind, as he preferred to pace the floor.

As the last of the students filed out of the room, McClarren observed them, making sure there were no stragglers. When he seemed satisfied that no one was slowing down or staying behind, he looked to Mackenzie and gave her a contemplative look.

"Would you consider yourself reliable?" he asked.

Confused, she bit back a startled smile. "I suppose I would," she answered.

"Good. Because I'm going to rely on you to keep the next five minutes or so a secret. I want no one to know that we ever had the discussion we are about to have. Do you understand me, Ms. White?"

"Yes, sir," she said. It was intimidating to be standing so close to him and to have him looking directly at her. Knowing the sorts of men he had worked with and the ways he had figured them out made her feel as if he could reach right into her head and pick out each and every one of her thoughts.

"From time to time, I still hear things," McClarren said. "Foolish men within the Bureau still consider me a confidant, I suppose. And one of the things I'm hearing lately is that you've been inserted into what has become quite the nasty dilemma. Is that correct?"

Mackenzie wasn't sure how to respond. Was this a test? Was he maybe prodding her at the request of McGrath or one of the men that worked under him?

"I don't know that I'm at liberty to say," she said.

"Ah, the expected answer from someone that has been pulled to and fro by the powers that be," he said with a satisfied smile. "Well then, let me see if this story sounds familiar to you. Let's say a young, promising lady comes through the Academy—so good and with such an impressive background that some of the directors and big wigs within the Bureau take notice. And let's also say they need to fill an empty slot suddenly left behind by a seasoned agent's partner." He stopped, smiled at her, and added: "Is this starting to sound familiar?"

"I might have heard of such a thing," Mackenzie said.

McClarren dropped the charade like an actor switching characters. "Listen," he said. "I know what was asked of you and I know that you were pulled away from it yesterday. I understand the thinking behind the idea but, quite frankly, I personally feel that the way you were discarded was a travesty. If they're going to put you in the game, they need to leave you there until the game is done. But that's just my feeling."

"Thank you, sir. I appreciate that."

"And I appreciate your situation," McClarren said. "That's why I'd like to help if I can. Under the radar, of course."

"Of course," Mackenzie repeated.

"Now, I know enough about the case to offer the merest of insights. But from what I can gather, the suspect is likely a man. He's discarding the victims like trash, but because the victims are both male and female, there are elements that must be considered that would not be considered in a typical case involving a sexual motive. So as of right now, I say you don't even consider motive. I say you focus on the sort of man these people might know. You see, more often than not, a repeated crime scene indicates a sort of familiarity. I believe the killer either knows these people or there is something about these people that *seems* familiar to him. Perhaps there is a link among the people he has killed and not between the victims and the killer. Have you considered that?"

"I have," she said. "But there's no obvious link. There's someone at the Bureau looking at genealogical aspects, but—"

"Oh, it's not family related," McClarren interrupted. "If it was, it would have been much clearer by the killer. There's intent there, a need for other family members to see what he has done. No…I believe what you are dealing with is a methodical man….a man that plans his killings."

"And that insight is based on the fact that he dumps the bodies at the same locations?" she asked.

"Yes. So if I were you, I'd ignore the man himself for now. Just study the victims."

"Well, like you said…I've been removed from the case."

"And?" he said. "If you just happen to come up with an idea that is far too good to be ignored, it's on the shoulders of the men currently ignoring you. I can guarantee you that they'd listen because if you suggest something that they ignore but turns out to be right…things could get very bad for them. Of course, I never suggested a thing to you because, as we summed up earlier, we are not having this conversation."

"Yes sir."

"The one other thing I thought was interesting…in the notes I saw, I read where you had apparently made the suggestion that the people were being held or contained in some sort of cage or entrapment based on the puncture wounds and scratches along the top of the head. It made me think of stray animals…cats and dogs that sympathetic families take in."

He stopped talking here, giving her the chance to connect the dots. She did so, a theory slowly falling into place.

"Strays," she said, thinking out loud. "Animals that wander around and willingly go to strangers, hoping for refuge."

He smiled. "Indeed."

"So maybe the killer isn't going to the victims…maybe…oh my God."

"Yes? What is it?" McClarren asked, still smiling.

"I've held the theory that the victims were all going to him somehow," Mackenzie said, nearly in a daze.

He nodded.

"Buy why—" she started, but was interrupted by a shake of McClarren's head.

Door-to-door, she thought, the idea now locking firmly in place. She knew then and there that it was the answer without any doubt.

"I'm sorry, Ms. White, but I don't see students after class unless it is by appointment." With this said, he gave her a little wink.

She offered him a quick smile in return and then headed quickly out of the room. By the time she reached the hallway, she was nearly in a sprint. With the door-to-door link now impossible to overlook, she felt like the entire case was starting unfold before her and she was afraid that if she didn't get back to her apartment and hunker down in front of the case files, she'd lose it.

With that sense of urgency pushing her, Mackenzie rushed outside. By the time she made it to the street, she was nearly running.

CHAPTER TWENTY TWO

She was so sure of her hunch when she got to her apartment that she wasted no time. She threw her backpack down on the floor in front of the door and dashed to the coffee table where her laptop and case files were still sitting from yesterday afternoon. She grabbed up the file folder and dumped out the contents, scattering them over the coffee table and the couch.

She came to Trevor Simms's information, possibly the easiest to pinpoint. It had all but been confirmed that he had spent the day he died out on the streets trying to land customers for his lawn care business. She then pulled out Dana Moore's information. While they had concrete confirmation about a door-to-door situation, her mother had indicated that much of her business was conducted by going to the homes of her potential customers.

Susan Kellerman wasn't a lock for the door-to-door theory, but some quick Google research could answer that question. She powered on her laptop and while she waited for it to come to the home screen, she looked over the scant information on Shanda Elliot—the first victim and the one they knew the least about.

She looked to the next of kin information in the case file and saw that her husband was listed. Finding out there was a door-to-door connection would be easy enough, but she was going to have to take a risk.

"To hell with it," she said, grabbing her cell phone.

Slowly, deliberately, she punched in the husband's number. She listened to it ring, praying it did not go to voicemail. She was already putting her ass on the line; leaving a voice message to call her back that could be used as physical evidence against her later on was simply *asking* for trouble.

Fortunately, it did not come to that. Tony Elliot answered on the third ring. "Hello?"

"Hi, is this Tony Elliot?" she asked.

"It is. Who is this?"

"Mr. Elliot, my name is Mackenzie White. I'm a consultant with the FBI and I've been asked to follow up on a few questions concerning your wife. We have what appears to be a promising lead on capturing the suspect but could use your help. Do you have a moment?"

"Yeah, I have a few minutes," he said. "What can I help you with?"

"Well, a lot of it is basically going to be things you may already have been asked. But we're double-checking everything right now."

"Is that bad?" he asked somberly.

"Not at all. We just have to be very efficient before settling on a lead and going in a certain direction with the investigation."

"Good, good," Tony Elliot said.

"Mr. Elliot, what did your wife do for a living?"

"She was a waitress at Ruby Tuesday's."

Just like that, Mackenzie's theory crumbled apart and hope deflated in her chest. She struggled to come up with a few more questions so the call wouldn't seem suspicious.

"And...what was the relationship with her employees like?"

"I don't know," he said. "She never really talked about them. The people she *did* talk about, though, were some of the weird people she met while working what she referred to as her second job."

"A second job?"

Tony sighed. "Yeah. If you can call it that. I think she averaged about sixty bucks a month with it."

"And what *was* her second job?"

"Avon," he said. "She tried selling Avon products on the side, hoping to help pay some bills."

Mackenzie's heart pounded.

Door to door.

"And did she go door-to-door for that?"

"Sometimes. She never really told me when she was going to do it, though. It always caused fights between us. She had to spend money to get the stuff and then never sold it. I think she even...,"

He trailed off here, as if struck by something.

"What is it, Mr. Elliot?"

"Hold on a second, would you?"

"Of course," she said, curious.

As she waited for him to come back on the line, she grabbed her laptop and started multi-tasking. With her phone held between her chin and shoulder, she pulled up the web browser on her laptop and typed in the name of Dana Moore's business: Natural Health Remedies. With such a generic name, numerous entries came up, so she narrowed it down with the geographic location and Dana's name.

A well-polished website popped up, featuring a beautiful picture of Dana Moore. Mackenzie scrolled to the *Contact Me* page and read the brief text. There, located at the bottom of the page, were two sentences: *If you have questions about my products or services, feel free to call and request a face-to-face consultation absolutely free! I'll even come straight to your front door!*

Mackenzie read the sentences several times, feeling her theory get a bit stronger. As she read through them for the third time, Tony Elliot's voice filled her ear again.

"Ms. White, are you still there?" he asked.

"I am."

"I feel so stupid," he said. "I never even thought to look before."

"Look for what?"

"Well...Shanda kept her Avon kit in the bedroom closet. She only moved it when she was going out for sales. Any other time, it stayed right there."

"And where is it now?" Mackenzie asked.

"Well, that's just the thing. It's gone. She must have been on an Avon call on the day she was killed."

CHAPTER TWENTY THREE

It was 2:05 when Mackenzie pulled her car into the parking garage of the J. Edgar Hoover building. She drove to the lowest level and parked in the far backside of the lot. There was already another car sitting there, parked in the shadows. She could see Bryers through the windshield. He looked irritated and a little worried.

Mackenzie quickly got out of her car, bringing her case files with her. She then walked over to the car Bryers was sitting in and got into the passenger seat. He looked at her in the same way a disappointed father might look at a daughter that had gotten in trouble at school.

"Thanks for meeting me," Mackenzie said. "I know you're risking a lot."

"You're damned right I am," he said. "So please tell me this game-changing discovery you've made."

"Well, I feel stupid because I'd offhandedly mentioned the possibility after we met with Caleb Kellerman. I should have pushed harder but I didn't want to step on anyone's toes. But I am now almost one hundred percent certain that our killer did not hunt down his victims. I'm pretty sure they went directly to him."

"And why would they do that?" Bryers asked. "You still pushing this door-to-door thing?"

"Yes, I am. They went to him because they were called there. They went of their own free will. If you looked really closely at the personal details, each and every one of the victims worked at least minutely in a door-to-door capacity."

"Go on," Bryers said. He wasn't being condescending. She knew he had bought into the door-to-door connection when she had first mentioned it. Now that she had a bit more to go on, he was apparently willing to look it over once more.

She opened her file and went through it page by page, handing each sheet to Bryers as she went through them.

"We know for a fact that Trevor Simms was going door-to-door for his business on the day he went missing. That's a fact. The unfortunate thing is that the log for that day was torn from his planner, so we have no idea where he was.

"Then there's Susan Kellerman. While her main job was usually working behind a desk and answering phones for A New You University, her husband told us that she sometimes went out on sales calls. He never got specific about the nature of the calls, but some very quick research showed me that about half of those calls are door-to-door.

"Next, Dana Moore. While we have no absolute proof that she was visiting a client for a visit on the day she was killed, the fact remains that a large portion of her clientele came about from her going door-to-door.

"And then the last one, which was totally overlooked: Shanda Elliot."

"She wasn't overlooked," Bryers said a bit defensively. "She was a waitress, right?"

"Yes, she was. But I spoke with her husband and—"

"When?"

"About an hour and a half ago."

"Damn it, White! Are you *trying* to get expelled?"

"No. I'm, *trying* to solve this case and keep more people from getting killed."

Bryers slammed his hand on the dash and cast her a look that actually hurt her a bit. He looked disappointed and angry but, deep down, curious. As if to confirm the curiosity, he gripped the edge of the dash and sighed.

"What did the husband have to say?"

"That Shanda sold Avon on the side. She made hardly anything on it and it was a point of contention in the marriage. He said she had a kit that she kept in the closet, only moving it when she was visiting someone for a call."

"Let me guess," Bryers said, the anger quickly flushing from his mood. "The kit isn't there, is it?"

"No. And he's pretty certain it was there the day before Shanda went missing."

Bryers nervously rubbed at the bridge of his nose and gave her another perplexed look. "That's some good work," he said. "Not airtight or bulletproof, but the best lead we have so far. But here's the thing...I need to present it to McGrath...and he's going to want to know how I made the connection. I can't *not* tell him you called the Elliot husband."

Mackenzie smiled nervously and looked upward. "His office is right over our heads, right?" she asked. "I say we pay him a visit."

"That might not be the best idea for you."

"Well, the last idea I had that wasn't good for me gave us this lead. So I'm willing to take my chances."

Bryers shrugged. "Whatever you want, White. It's your funeral."

CHAPTER TWENTY FOUR

McGrath's eyes were narrow and thin, like a man squinting from the pain of an incredibly bad headache. He sat quietly, looking across his desk at Mackenzie and Bryers. They had just presented him with Mackenzie's findings and in the fifteen seconds that had passed, McGrath had not spoken a single word.

In a sudden motion, McGrath pushed his chair back from his desk and got to his feet. He didn't really look mad, but he certainly wasn't happy, either.

"You understand," he finally said, looking at Mackenzie, "that this is grounds for severe punishment. The simplest punishment would be to simply expel you from the Academy. Not only did you go directly against my orders, but you basically also assumed the identity of a consultant for the Bureau—a title you were revoked of when I pulled you off of the case.

"And you," he said, now swinging like a pendulum toward Bryers, "should have known better than to take her call. You knew she had been pulled from the case and the smartest thing you could have done would to have been to ignore the call."

"With all due respect, sir," Bryers said, "I answered the call because she's smart and I value her opinion. More than that, I am also very much aware that she was pulled into a nearly impossible situation and, despite that, performed well—albeit a bit like an anxious rookie…which she is."

"Watch your tone, Agent Bryers," McGrath said.

Bryers nodded, but went on. "Also, I might add that *because* I took her call, we now have the strongest lead on this case that we've managed to—"

"I know how strong the fucking lead is," McGrath said, stuck somewhere between resigned defeat and absolute frustration. "And that's why, against my much better judgment, I have decided to put her back on the case."

"What?" Mackenzie asked in utter disbelief.

McGrath leaned across his desk and leveled his gaze at her. She could feel his fury coming at her in waves but she also sensed a sort of wavering hope there as well.

"This time, you do everything you're told," he sneered. "You play by the rules and you work as quietly and as unnoticed as you can. You're a ghost, you understand? No one else outside of this room knows about this decision. And that means if you *should* crack this case, you won't be recognized. It will be passed to Bryers or whatever other agent might be closest to you if a capture goes down. Am I understood?"

"Yes, sir."

"Good. Now…as you're officially back on this case, tell me where you'd go from here, feeling confident that this man is killing people that go door-to-door."

"There are a few avenues," she said. "But I think the two best leads are going to come from Dana Moore and Trevor Simms. With Dana Moore, we'd need access to her e-mail and computers, looking for scheduled calls or visits. With Trevor Simms, we could speak with his co-worker to find out what neighborhoods they had discussed as potential customer targets. I also think we should consider the Black Mill Street area, since we have confirmation from the bus driver that Susan Kellerman was headed that way on the day she disappeared. Becka Rudolph also said that she was pretty sure Dana Moore planned to visit that area. "

McGrath considered this for a moment and sighed. "I'm okay with you speaking with the friends and family of Trevor Simms. But stay away from Becka Rudolph. That woman hated you, apparently. As for Black Mill Street, I'll send someone over to canvass the area. Once you've exhausted your resources for Trevor Simms, I'll have you and Bryers head over to Black Mill to help with the search."

"Yes, sir. And…thank you."

"Don't you dare thank me yet," McGrath said. "Just get out there and prove to me that I'm not a complete moron by giving you this second chance."

Mackenzie gave a quick nod and headed out of the office. After a few moments, she heard Bryers falling in behind her. When they were safely away from McGrath's office and hurrying down the hallway for the elevator, Mackenzie realized that she had somehow gotten sucked right back into the whirlwind.

As they waited for the elevator at the end of the hallway, Mackenzie drew up as much courage as she could before speaking to Bryers. She'd always found it hard to be genuinely open and thankful; it made her feel awkward and indebted to someone.

"Thanks for what you did in there," she said. "You didn't have to stand up for me like that."

"No need to thank me," Bryers said. "And don't get used to it. It's not too often that someone will go to bat for you like that. I just thought you deserved it, given the absolutely wretched situation you were dealt."

She wanted to add that no one had ever stood up for her like that—not as a detective in Nebraska, not in her family during her childhood, not even in high school when she had relied heavily on her friends for encouragement and support she was not getting at home.

But she kept that quiet. There was no sense in opening up those sorts of wounds and invitations to pain. So instead, she waited in silence with him until the elevator arrived with a *ding* that seemed to invite her back into the hunt for a killer that was somehow luring his victims directly to his front door.

CHAPTER TWENTY FIVE

Lauren Wickline did not like talking in front of people. In fact, whenever she was in a crowd of friends that equaled more than ten, she usually stayed quiet. Last year, during her sophomore year of high school, she'd had to speak in front of the entire freshman class to welcome them to the school and she nearly barfed all over the place. Speaking to large groups of people was simply not her thing. One or two people, though—that's where she really shined. That's why it seemed like such a perfect fit to be a representative for the girls' track and field team.

She was peddling discount booklets for local businesses, trying to raise money for the team so they could finally get some decent uniforms. So far, the door-to-door approach had worked wonderfully. She knew she had a charming smile and, for the horny old men that answered the door, a rack that even college girls would die for, much less her friends in high school. So when she had to, Lauren knew the ways to bend or lean in order to make a sale.

She was currently walking up Estes Street, a block over from a part of town their coaches had told them to avoid. Black Mill Street had gotten a bad reputation; it was so bad that even the druggies and stoners at school had stopped buying drugs from the area. And even though Lauren knew for herself that it could be a dangerous place, she also knew that it was the middle of the afternoon and that if she played her cards right (and her cleavage, of course) she could make more money that anyone else on the team and finally be recognized as an actual contributor rather than the pretty girl that all the guys come to the meets to check out.

She had four houses left and, after going door-to door on more than twenty houses, had sold seven of the booklets—not a great haul but more than she had been expecting in this neighborhood. She was also making great time. She'd left school early and knew that if she could wrap things up within the next half an hour or so, she'd be able to make it back to practice with this unexpected chunk of money.

She approached the next sidewalk and started to get that tingling in her stomach, the old familiar pangs of nervousness. She'd gotten it a few times while selling the booklets but always managed to swallow it down. It wasn't so much about speaking to strangers, but the embarrassment of peddling something that they had no real interest in.

Just four houses left, she thought to herself. *Just get over yourself and get it done. Get it done with enough time to get back to practice, deliver the money, and bask in the praise of the coach and the other runners.*

That thought quickened her step. She walked up the sidewalk and knocked on the front door with confidence. Right away, from somewhere inside, she heard a man say rather loudly: *"You stay put, Mom! I got it."*

The man's voice sounded a little off...maybe sort of excited or nervous. Had he maybe spied her coming up the sidewalk in her athletic shorts and tight-fitting T-shirt? She didn't really care one way or the other. A sale was a sale.

Seconds later, the front door was opened. A man that looked to be in his forties or so looked out at her. His gaze was at first curious and then somewhere near amazed. What confused Lauren, though, was that he was not staring at her like most men his age did. There was something else in his gaze—something that Lauren did not like at all.

"Hello?" the man said in an almost breathless voice.

No way, she thought, gripping the booklets tightly in her hand. *This guy is a creep. This guy is bad news and no sale is worth this. Move your ass, Lauren.*

"Sorry," she said. "Wrong house."

"It's okay," the man said. "Are you lost?"

No," Lauren said, shaking her head. "Sorry to bother you."

She turned away quickly and stepped toward the stairs.

That's when she felt the man grab her by the messy bun of hair in the back of her head. She felt her head whipped backward quickly and then a massive arm fell around her chest. She tried to let out a scream for help but then a sweaty hand was locked firmly around her mouth.

Lauren kicked madly, trying to free herself as she felt herself pulled through the front door and into the house. The world spun as she was thrown to the floor and then the man was there, his hands on her in a way that was not sexual but somehow far, *far* worse.

When his hand came off of her mouth, she tried to scream again but then his other hand came out of nowhere. It struck her hard in the side of the head.

And brought with it a sheet of darkness.

CHAPTER TWENTY SIX

As it turned out, speaking to Trevor Simms's co-worker and part owner of The Green Team did not take long at all. Benjamin Worley had already spoken to the police and the Bureau very briefly following the discovery of Trevor's body. In his records, there were notes about the neighborhoods that Trevor had mentioned canvassing on the day he went missing. When Mackenzie called him, he reestablished those locations and made himself readily available to answer more questions or help in any way he could.

Unable to make herself return to her apartment, Mackenzie had made the phone call from her car, still parked in the parking garage beneath the J. Edgar Hoover building. With the neighborhoods written down, Mackenzie then pulled up a map of the area on her phone. After a few moments of scrolling around the map, she got the confirmation she needed.

One of the streets Trevor Simms had planned to visit was Estes Street. Estes Street just happened to be two streets over from Black Mill Street. The streets were simply too close together to be a coincidence. As far as she was concerned, every single clue in this case was pointing back to Black Mill Street.

She started her car and called Bryers on her way out of the parking garage. He answered right away, sounding just as excited as Mackenzie felt.

"Got something?" he asked.

"Yes. One of the places Trevor Simms had scheduled to visit was Estes Street. That's two blocks over from Black Mills."

"How soon can you be over there?" Bryers asked.

"I'm already on the way."

"Just please remember what McGrath said. You have to stay invisible on this, okay?"

"I know," Mackenzie said, suddenly starting to resent it.

"Why don't you meet me at the corner of Black Mill and Sawyer Street? We can start from there. I don't know when McGrath is going to have others over there."

"Sounds good," she said. "See you then."

Mackenzie ended the call and focused on the traffic. It was quickly reaching four o'clock in the afternoon. Soon, the afternoon rush would clog up the main roads. It wasn't until then, as she merged off of the central roads and onto the freeway, that Mackenzie realized that a sensation she'd felt about three months ago while on the heels of the Scarecrow Killer was washing over her.

It was the feeling that she was suddenly racing against the clock, not quite sure which hour could be the last.

***

She pulled her car along the curb several feet away from the intersection of Black Mill and Sawyer twenty-five minutes later. Apparently, Bryers also felt as if they were racing against the clock because he was already there, waiting for her. He flashed his brake lights at her, signaling for her to come join him. She did so quickly, locking her car up and once again hopping into his passenger seat.

"Have you ever done this before?" Bryers asked her. He looked anxious and a bit nervous. More than that, he looked tired and maybe even borderline sick.

"A few times," she said. "Going door to door looking for a missing kid and then again in the hopes of finding a coke dealer."

"So...you know that at any moment, we can knock on a door and be met with force?"

"Yes," she said.

Quickly, Bryers reached over and thumbed open the glovebox. When it fell open, Mackenzie saw a neatly organized space with maps, vehicle ID, a small toolbox, and a Glock 26—a small handgun that she'd heard some students in the Academy refer to as a Baby Glock. It was roughly half the size of a standard Glock, easy to conceal, and a little toy-like in its appearance, but it could still get the job done.

"Take it," Bryers said. "McGrath doesn't need to know. But I'll be damned if I'm going to let you walk into this without protection."

"Are you sure?" she asked, already reaching for it.

"No. So take it quickly. And then check the trunk which I'm about to *accidentally* pop for a small-of-back holster."

Without looking away from her, he reached down and to his left, popping the trunk. She stepped out of the car, went to the trunk, and found the back holster stowed away in a small kit with a few other holster-related items. She then turned her back to the car, trying to look inconspicuous to anyone that might pass by, as she holstered the gun and then attached the holster to the inside of the waist of her jeans. She'd never worn a small-of-back holster; she arched her back a bit to get used to the shape of it.

Bryers joined her at the back of the car and looked up the street. "I say we start here, on Black Mill," he said. "Maybe just cover a few blocks. After that, if we don't find anything, I think we head over to Estes since that's one of the streets Trevor Simms specifically named. We go together, never apart. I hate to make you feel like you're being babysat, but—"

"It's okay," she said. "I get it."

A curt little nod from Bryers told her that he'd not mention it again. With that, he started walking forward, beyond the intersection and to the scattered houses ahead. The streets were empty for the most part. As they made their way forward, Mackenzie saw an afternoon jogger sprinting across an intersection further ahead, but that was about it.

They came to their first home, a sad-looking shack of a place with a mostly dislodged satellite antennae dangling from the roof. The grass had clearly not been mown in about a month and the house's vinyl siding was in desperate need of a pressure washing. As she and Bryers walked up the cracked sidewalk to the front door, Mackenzie prepared herself for how this task would go. As she'd told Bryers, she'd done it before; she knew the next hour or so would consist of having doors answered by cranky people or no people at all, with startled noisy dogs on the other side.

They approached the first house and Bryers knocked on the door. The sound was abrupt and hollow in the silence of the neighborhood. They waited a beat, exchanging a knowing glance, and then Bryers tried again. As they waited this time, Mackenzie looked to the window by the front door, looking for any signs of movement. But as far as she could tell, no one was spying on them through the dingy curtains.

"No one's home," Bryers said after another thirty seconds of waiting. "On to the next."

They left the house and walked just a few yards before coming to the next one and getting the same result. At the third, however, someone was home. When Bryers knocked, the door was answered by a man that was either sick or drunk. It took less than ten seconds for Mackenzie to determine that not only was this man not a suspect, but that he'd be absolutely no help in terms of questioning. After an awkward exchange where half of the man's words were slurred and incomprehensible, they headed on to the next house.

After two more empty homes, they came to a small house that looked relatively tidy from the outside. As they walked up the sidewalk, Mackenzie spotted a television through the front window. It was turned at an angle but she could see that a talk show was currently filling the screen. Whoever was watching it, though, was apparently sitting away from the window.

They approached the front door showing the first signs of fatigue and disappointment from what was starting to seem like a pointless errand. Bryers knocked as usual and they could hear movement from behind the door within a matter of seconds.

Eventually, a waifish older woman came to the door. Her hair was almost entirely gray and her skin was loose and wrinkled. Mackenzie guessed the woman to be in her late seventies or so. She regarded them both with a pair of thick glasses that she pushed up onto her nose.

"Yes? Can I help you?"

"Sorry to bother you, ma'am," Bryers said, showing his badge. "I'm Agent Bryers with the FBI. We're staking out the neighborhood, looking for a certain individual or anyone that might be able to provide information."

The old lady nodded solemnly, as if she had been expecting their visit but they had taken too long to get there. "Well, it's about damned time," she said.

"What does that mean?" Bryers asked.

The old woman took a step out onto her concrete slab of a porch and looked to her right, in the direction Mackenzie and Bryers had been heading this whole time. She extended a bony finger, pointing to a house two yards down.

"There's a very bad man that lives there. I've called the police about it twice but they have never done anything about it."

"What sort of bad man, ma'am?" Bryers asked.

"People are coming and going out of that house all of the time," she said. "Mostly late at night. A lot of time, there are little girls."

"Little girls?"

"Well, not *little*. Thirteen or fourteen, I'd guess. And the man that lives there…well, there's no need for him to have girls that age at his house."

"Maybe they are his daughters?" Mackenzie suggested.

"Of course they aren't," the woman spat. "Not unless he has *lots* of daughters. And these girls…they look like they're being escorted—"

"Do you know this man's routine?" Bryers asked. "Is he home right now?"

"He keeps his car parked along the side of the house," the old woman said. "If it's there, so is he. Now, I know I sound like some nosy old biddy, but I *know* there's something bad that goes on there."

"Thank you, ma'am," Bryers said, looking in the direction of the house. "We'll check it out."

"Good," the old woman said.

Bryers and Mackenzie went back to the sidewalk and headed down toward the house the old woman had pointed out. "You believe her?" Mackenzie asked.

"I don't know. But it's certainly worth checking out. Don't you think?"

Mackenzie nodded even though something about the situation didn't feel quite right. If this guy was guilty of anything that involved young girls, there was a chance that it was purely sexual. Illegal and morbid, of course, but it was not an MO that lined up with the man she believed they were looking for.

Still, after knocking on the door of the house next to the old lady and finding no one home, they ventured to the house in question. As the old woman had indicated, there was a car parked alongside the house, partially off of the faded paved driveway. They both gave it only a glance as they walked across the yard and to the front porch. The porch was a dirty little square of wood and shadow, littered with cigarette butts, dead insects, and grime.

"Ready?" Bryers asked.

She nodded her confirmation. Suddenly, she was very aware of the Baby Glock holstered at her back.

Bryers raised his hand and knocked. They waited a moment, listening for the sounds of movement. Mackenzie heard a slight shuffling noise but was fairly certain it was not coming from inside.

It was *outside*. And if her ears were picking the noise up correctly, she was pretty sure the sound was coming from the back.

"You hear that?" she asked.

"No," Bryers said. "What is it?"

Mackenzie waited a moment, making sure she could still hear the sound. When she continued to hear it, she wasted no time running for the porch steps.

"Around back," she said. "Someone's making a run for it."

CHAPTER TWENTY SEVEN

As she dashed across the side yard and to the small backyard beyond, she remembered McGrath's order to be like a ghost. Be invisible. Be in the background and out of the way. She knew that chasing after someone as they attempted to escape through the back door was directly disobeying that order but in the moment, she didn't know what else to do.

Just as she heard Bryers falling in behind her, she caught sight of two men at the edge of the backyard. The yard fed into a small strangled field that ran on for a bit before the backyard to another property took over. As Mackenzie's eyes fell on the two men, they were running across the small field, heading west. One of them spotted her as she rounded the corner of the house into the backyard and this seemed to kick him into a higher gear.

Mackenzie knew she was fast and had better-than-average endurance. She was confident that she could catch up to the men. But then what? She had Bryers's Baby Glock holstered at her back but if she drew it, McGrath would have her ass.

She turned quickly back to Bryers, desperate for some sort of confirmation or approval. "Can you catch up to them?" she asked.

He frowned, watching the two men get further away from them with every second. Seeing him at a dead sprint, she could tell that he was struggling.

"Doubtful," he said.

Mackenzie looked back towards the men and gave a grunt of frustration.

"White?" Bryers said. "Don't even—"

But she was already moving. Her legs instantly found the refined speed that they'd gathered over the last six weeks as she'd run through obstacle courses and wooded trails. The only thing different about it now was that her muscles were practically soaked in adrenaline as she bolted across the backyard and toward the field. Behind her, she barely heard Bryers let out a strangled curse. Without bothering to look over her shoulder, Mackenzie knew that he was following along, trying to keep up with her.

With each running stride she took closer to the field and the rushing shapes of the two men ahead of her, she felt her future crumbling. She knew that this was a no-win situation and for a moment, she despised the men that had organized back room meetings to essentially place her in the situation. If she'd seen the two men escaping and *didn't* give chase, she'd be seen as a failure.

On the other hand, chasing after them was going against everything McGrath had instructed her to do.

She figured she'd sort through all of that when all was said and done. For now, she had a man that had potentially killed at least four people on the run. And she'd be damned if she was going to let him get away.

She was running with such fury that she nearly stumbled when her feet stepped off of the smooth grass of the yard onto the thick tangles mess of the dead field. She regained her balance quickly, though, and peered ahead to see the two men coming to the end of the field and cutting through someone else's backyard. They were faster than she had given them credit for and she was going to have a chase on her hand if she stumbled again.

She finally got a chance to catch a glimpse of Bryers as she made it into the field. He was about twenty yards behind her, running with purpose but obviously not accustomed to the exertion. She then refocused on the men ahead of her and again slipped into the zone she'd found so comfortable while getting accustomed to the Academy's rigorous training. She ran hard, her legs not tired, her lungs working like some perfect machine.

She lost sight of the two men for a moment but kept her eyes glued on the yard that they had escaped into. It was coming up fast on her right, a dry patch of grass behind a ramshackle house. An old clothesline and rusty swing set sat in the yard. As she scanned the yard, trying to take everything in at once while still running, she barely caught sight of the flurry of motion coming from the far side of the house.

One of the two men had stopped, hiding behind the house. He was now rushing at her, his shoulders low and head tucked in almost like a linebacker. She stopped in her tracks, her feet coming to a skidding halt. As she repositioned herself and turned to the left, she knew she wouldn't have time to pull Bryers's gun. Instead, she clutched her hands together into one big fist, raised her arms and the brought them down like a club.

She made contact just as the man's thick shoulder collided with her stomach. The wind went racing out of her as she went to the ground. Still, she had landed a solid blow just below the man's neck and when they collapsed to the ground, he was grunting in pain and instantly trying to get to his feet.

Mackenzie scrambled to her own feet, fighting to draw in a breath of air. She was much faster than him and by the time she was on her feet, he had barely made it into a crouching position. She launched herself at him in a tackle that sent him back to the ground face first. Wasting no time, she threw a hard knee into the small of his back and then pressed her forearm into the back of his neck as hard as she was able.

When he tried fighting her off, she pressed her knee harder into his back and her forearm harder into his neck. It was a simple yet effective hold—one of the first she had learned. Any attempt to break free of her was going to result in severe back pain or scratches and abrasions to the face.

"Where's the other one?" Mackenzie asked as he struggled beneath her. "Where's your friend?"

"Fuck you," came the answer.

She put more weight on her knee in response. He grunted out in pain beneath her and tried using his arms to push himself up. Mackenzie reached out and took his left arm, drawing it back behind him. He was slammed into the ground as she bent his arm upwards along his back. He let out another strangled cry that was mostly drowned out by the sound of Bryers rushing up to her side. He was out of breath and red in the face as he dropped to his knees beside her.

"I got him," he said as he pulled a pair of cuffs from his belt.

When he set the cuffs to the man's wrists, he seemed to pay Mackenzie very little attention. He even bumped into her as he worked, nearly knocking her off of the suspect and onto the ground. Sensing that he was clearly irritated, Mackenzie stepped away and got to her feet as Bryers hauled the man up.

"Want me to go after the other one?" Mackenzie asked.

"No," Bryers spat, clearly upset. He then shook the cuffed man and got into his face. "Where'd the other one go?"

The man only shrugged. The expression in his face was one of worry but it was also evident that he was going to be stubborn.

"Was that your house or his?" Bryers asked, nodding back the way they had come from.

Again, the man said nothing. He simply stared from Bryers to Mackenzie and then back to Bryers.

"So we're just going to let him go?" Mackenzie asked.

The cuffed man smiled at this. He shot Mackenzie an utter look of contempt. He was rewarded with Bryers getting in his face again and returning the smile.

"Something funny? Seems to me that you'd be a little scared of a woman that just handed you your ass."

This wiped the smile from the man's face. He simply looked to the ground as Bryers guided him back toward the field. Mackenzie followed, feeling a heavy wave of uncertainty wash over her while Bryers was clearly sorting through his own thoughts.

"Got your phone on you?" he asked her suddenly.

"Yes."

"Call this in to McGrath. Tell him I took the suspect down and we have another one on the loose. Then tell him we need a warrant for the house this upstanding citizen ran out of."

"That ain't my house, man," the cuffed man said.

"Finally, it speaks," Bryers said.

Mackenzie took out her phone and pulled up McGrath's number as they walked back across the dead field and returned to the house in question. Even before the phone started to ring, Mackenzie started to feel certain of two things. One: the cuffed man's instant remark of *that ain't my house* meant that there was something there that was going to cause *someone* a hell of a lot of trouble. Two: neither of these men was the killer they were looking for.

Their killer seemed methodical and almost predictable. Someone like that would have a plan in place for an easy and foolproof escape should the cops ever come knocking; she didn't think he'd be the type to simply sneak out the back door and run.

Of course, she was going to keep these things to herself until they saw the inside of the house. If she was vocal about her gut instinct and turned out to be wrong, there was no telling how it could skew the way McGrath and Bryers thought of her.

So for now, she simply reported recent events to McGrath as she marched back down the field with Bryers and the cuffed suspect. And even though they technically had a suspect in custody, Mackenzie could still not shake the feeling that there was a ticking clock still pushing her from behind.

CHAPTER TWENTY EIGHT

The last thing she had expected was for McGrath to give her access to the house once the go-ahead had been given. She was also once again surprised with how quickly everything had moved. Less than an hour passed between her making the call and a small team arriving at the house on Black Mill Street. She had a feeling that Bryers had pushed for her inclusion in the search but did not ask. She simply did as she was told and joined the team of four agents on the small front porch of the last house they had visited in their search of the neighborhood.

She stayed close to Bryers as the door was taken down by a small battering ram. The door fell in easily, hanging on by the stubborn top hinge. Mackenzie stood back as two agents took the lead, armed with simple Glocks. They took a moment to clear the place, making sure no one was lurking around the corners with weapons, waiting to ambush them.

"Clear!" one of them called.

Bryers nodded to Mackenzie and she followed behind him, bringing up the rear. She had no gun now, as Bryers had taken the Baby Glock off of her after she'd made the call to McGrath. She'd already disobeyed the command to be a ghost and Bryers wasn't about to push his luck by allowing her to remain armed on a case she wasn't even supposed to be a part of.

Bringing up the rear of the small group, Mackenzie took in the house like any visitor would. The front door led into a spacious living room, the center of which was adorned by a huge flat-screen TV on the wall. It had been left on during the escape, the screen showing a Netflix menu with action films. A nearly full beer bottle sat on a small coffee table in front of the couch.

They walked through the living room and into an adjoining kitchen. A few dishes were piled up in the sink. A bag of chips sat open on the counter. A bottle of vodka sat by the sink with a few shot glasses scattered here and there.

From the kitchen, they ventured into the hallway where the house's single bathroom and two bedrooms started to give the first indicators that something despicable *had* indeed been taking place within these walls.

In the bathroom, the first signs of authenticity to the nosy old neighbor's claims presented themselves. An empty box of condoms was in the trashcan along with prescription bottles of oxycodone and several boxes of Ambien. There were also a few empty beer cans in the trash which by themselves meant nothing, but in tandem with the oxycodone and Ambien did not paint a pretty picture.

In the first bedroom—the master, it seemed—the bed was unmade, the sheets in a heap at the foot of the bed. On the bedside table was another prescription bottle of pills and velvet-lined handcuffs. In the floor, a pile of clothes was at first not even worth noticing until Mackenzie noticed a pink border around the sleeve of a shirt.

She kicked at the pile, not wanting to get her prints on anything. A pair of jeans tumbled from the pile, revealing a white shirt with a glittery star on the front. A series of pink lines ran across the sleeves. Without seeing the tag inside the collar, Mackenzie knew that the shirt belonged to a young girl—a twelve or thirteen year-old at most.

"Bryers," she said.

He turned and she pointed to it. His face went slack for a moment before he gave her a curt little nod and turned back toward the rest of the search. The small team of four went back into the hall where they checked the second bedroom. The room was essentially empty, with the exception of a small dresser and a mirror that was barely hanging to the wall. One of the agents in front of the group opened up a small closet along the back of the room and said, "Oh shit."

One by one, they stepped into the closet. What looked like a small closet from the outside actually opened up into a small room that was roughly ten feet long by five eight feet wide. All four of them stood inside of it shoulder to shoulder, nearly taking up the entire space. One of the agents pulled a cord hanging from the ceiling, turning on a single overhead bulb. It was a dim bulb, illuminating a scene similar to ones Mackenzie had heard about before but had never actually seen.

A small twin mattress lay on the floor. Another set of velvet-lined handcuffs lay on the floor next to it. A small mirror was affixed to the wall in front of the mattress. A My Little Pony blanket was bundled up in the corner beside a few discarded paper cups. One of the agents took up one of the cups and smelled it.

"Alcohol," he said.

All four of them were quiet. Mackenzie could practically feel their thoughts collectively whirling. Sure, there was not yet any *hard* proof that the neighbor had been right but everything they were seeing spelled it out for them.

The lead agent turned to Bryers. Mackenzie was impressed with the blank slate of his face. He showed no expression—no pity or rage or *anything.* "We're going to call in a team to scour the place for prints and anything else we can find. You good here?"

"Yeah. I think so."

The lead agent and his partner nodded and slowly backed out of the closet. As Bryers followed them, Mackenzie continued to peer into the closet. Bryers stood at the door, waiting for her.

"Don't do that to yourself," he said. "Right now we need to focus on getting the guy that got away."

"Yeah," Mackenzie said. She started to back away but as she did, she saw something that grabbed her attention. She stepped further into the closet and dropped into a hunched position just in front of the small mattress.

"What is it?" Bryers asked.

"Look," she said, reaching her hand out and nearly touching the small mirror on the wall.

In the bottom left corner, the glass was broken, revealing the thin metal backing. The spiraled end of a small screw stuck out about a quarter of an inch.

"What about it?" Bryers asked.

Mackenzie hated to say what was on her mind because it went against her strong feeling that this wasn't the killer. It was a deranged individual, sure...but not the guy that had been killing people going door-to-door and then throwing their bodies into dumpster.

"The scratch on top of Trevor Simms's head," she started.

"Oh," Bryers said. Then, after a few moments, he said it again, in a defeated tone. "Oh. You don't think this is our killer, do you?"

"This guy was after little girls," Mackenzie said. "And from what we've seen, he didn't kill them. He just...well, you know. Our guy, though...he's not picky. And his victims were adults."

"But the neighborhood is a match. And if this guy is *this* sick," he said, pointing into the closet, "there's no telling what else he's capable of."

"Yeah, but—"

"We have to go with what we have," Bryers interrupted. "And right now, this place is almost a surefire score. Relax, White. It's looking like we got our guy."

Mackenzie looked back to the closet, eyeing the screw, and knew without a doubt that he was wrong.

CHAPTER TWENTY NINE

By 5:30 that afternoon, the second man that had run from Mackenzie and Bryers was apprehended. The house belonged to him and it was becoming more and more clear that the neighbor's story had been pretty accurate. It had taken just the slightest bit of pressure and questioning to make his friend crack under the pressure, revealing that they worked together to acquire pre-teen and teenage girls for sex. Sometimes the parents were selling them, renting out their own daughters for anywhere between four hundred to one thousand dollars. But more often than not, the kids came of their own accord, rebelling against parents or seeking some sort of messed up security.

Neither of the men, however, fessed up to the deaths of Shanda Elliot, Susan Kellerman, Trevor Simms, or Dana Moore.

Less than ninety minutes after discovering the sordid closet, the suspect that had gotten away had been located, officially arrested, and headed for processing. Mackenzie sat on the steps of the house, watching the police car drive into the distance, slightly in awe of how quickly and efficiently it had all played out.

Bryers stood on the sidewalk, eager to head back to their cars. "You still don't feel good about it this, I take it?" he asked.

"I'm glad we got a creep that preys on young girls," she said. "That's a plus any day as far as I'm concerned. But this guy is not our dumpster killer."

Bryers sighed and nodded. "You might be right. But until I get an order from McGrath to keep looking for a suspect, we have to go with what we have. And what we have is a guy so screwed in the head that I wouldn't put *anything* past him."

"So even if you have a doubt…you can just let it go like that?" Mackenzie asked.

Bryers closed his eyes for a moment and Mackenzie could tell that he was trying to be diplomatic. When he spoke, his words were slow and deliberate.

"At the risk of coming off like a bastard…this isn't some shit-kicking PD in Nebraska. If you walk out of line in the Bureau, there are always consequences. We run a tight ship and there are rules to be followed. You get that, right?"

"I get it," she said. "We sit on our asses while waiting for McGrath to figure out that our killer is still out there."

"That's it, in a nutshell," Bryers said. "I suspect he already knows it. But he's going to make one hundred percent sure. I expect we'll get a heads-up tonight. But for now, we can't do much of anything other than get out of here. You did really well today, White. Leave it at that for now. Come on. Let's go."

Without waiting for her to respond, Bryers started down the sidewalk, back to where their cars were parked and waiting for them. It was a struggle, but Mackenzie did the same. She followed after Bryers and looked back to the house they'd just come out, and wondered for the first time if she'd made a mistake by taking Ellington's lead and leaving Nebraska.

* * *

When she was behind the wheel of her car and watching Bryers pull his own car out onto the street, Mackenzie discovered that she couldn't do it. She couldn't leave such a huge question unanswered. She would not be able to hold her head up high if she *knew* she had potentially left a killer on the loose when his place of residence could be within a mile of where she currently sat.

She cranked her car and made sure not to pull away from the curb before Bryers had already made his way through the intersection ahead. Another block forward and he'd take a left onto a street that led to a bypass that would take him back to Quantico. Mackenzie had no intention of following him.

She crept to the intersection he had passed through, hoping he saw her moving in his rearview. She stayed there for a moment until his car was out of sight.

And then she made a right.

Estes Street was one block over; she saw the green street sign even as she made the turn. It was the last known street Trevor Simms said he had been headed and it seemed insane to her to simply dismiss it because they had landed an impressive arrest twenty minutes ago.

She ran a quick circuit of the street, taking in its geography. It ran along for eight blocks before it ended in a decrepit roundabout at one end and changed into the busier Parks Avenue on the other. She drove back down Estes and parked at the intersection of Estes and Sawyer, starting within the same point she and Bryers had canvassed on Black Mill Street.

The neighborhood was nearly identical to what they had seen on Black Mill Street. A few of the homes were better maintained and most lawns were in better shape. Still, she felt nearly naked without a weapon. It was more than the fact that the neighborhood seemed shady and dangerous; it was the knowledge—the undeniable gut instinct—that told her that the dumpster killer lived in one of the houses that waited for her along Estes Street.

As she walked up the first sidewalk, she again sensed that she was perched upon a ledge that contained her future. She was aware that she could fall at any moment and that there were any number of supervisors and directors that could give her the push that would send her falling over at any moment. She felt the weight of this on her like a load of bricks on her back, but she pressed on anyway.

It was 5:50 in the afternoon when she knocked on her first door. It was answered within a few seconds by a middle-aged black gentleman. He was dressed in a mechanic's uniform and looked tired. He, like most others along Estes Street, had just gotten off of work, probably arriving home and seeing a commotion involving police cars on Black Mill Street.

"Yeah?" the man asked tiredly.

"I'm sorry to bother you," Mackenzie said, working on the sly. "I'm a consultant with the FBI. I don't know if you noticed the scene over on Black Mill, but we're canvassing the surrounding blocks in search of a man on the run. Have you happened to see anyone unfamiliar running through the yards or down the streets?"

The man shook his head. "Nope. I got home, cracked open a beer, and just about fell asleep on the couch. I ain't seen nothing."

Mackenzie nodded, quickly scanning the house behind him. She saw a living room and a hallway beyond. The house was clean and dark, a television murmuring somewhere from within.

"Thank you, sir," she said.

He only nodded at her and then closed the door. Mackenzie stepped down from his front steps and headed further down the street. She wondered how long it would take for Bryers to realize that she had stayed behind. A small part of her (perhaps the part that knew this disobedience could very well cost her a future within the FBI) wanted to switch her cell phone to silent so she'd conveniently not hear the phone if he called to ask just what in the hell she thought she was doing. But of course, that would be immature and she wasn't going to run away from the trouble she knew full well she was creating for herself.

So she continued to go door to door. Out of the first five doors she knocked on, three were answered. One was answered by a young girl, surely no older than twelve. Right away, Mackenzie could hear the sounds of the girl's parents arguing loudly in another room. The girl looked irritated and Mackenzie felt awkward over the whole ordeal. It was an awkwardness that she carried with her to the sixth house along the street, beginning to think that this whole thing had been a terrible idea on her part.

At the sixth house on her ill-advised search, she knocked on the door. She listened for motion on the other side and heard a woman's voice calling out. *"One minute!"*

Mackenzie waited twenty seconds or so before the door was answered. An older overweight woman answered the door. She looked tired and exhausted from simply coming to answer the door.

"Can I help you?" the woman asked with a tired yet cheerful tone.

Very quickly, Mackenzie gave the woman the same spiel she had given the other two adults she had spoken with in the last ten minutes. The woman looked concerned as Mackenzie filled her in but shook her head.

"No. I haven't seen anything like that," she said. "Then again, I'm usually back in my bedroom. I've been bedridden for a few weeks now. I haven't been feeling the best lately so I stay holed up back there."

"Sorry to hear it," Mackenzie said. Then, recalling how a very sensitive Becka Rudolph had complained that she was cold and distant, she added: "I hope the health problems aren't too serious."

"Not too bad," the woman said. "Nothing some healthy food and a better lifestyle won't change. I just really need to drop some of this weight." The lady said it in a way that made it clear she never truly expected to do such a thing.

"Well, I wish you the best," Mackenzie said. "Thank you for your time."

"Of course," the woman said. "I do hope you catch the man you're looking for."

Same here, Mackenzie said as she turned away from the woman and started back for the street.

As she took her first few steps, she thought she heard something…maybe nothing more than an additional thumping noise as the old woman gave her door a final push to close it. It was a muted noise, barely there at all.

You're jumping at the slightest noise, she told herself. *Don't make a fool of yourself.*

Still, Mackenzie stood there, motionless for a moment. She looked at the house, waiting to hear the sound again, but it never came.

What she *did* hear was her phone ringing in her pocket. She grabbed it and saw that it was Bryers.

"Shit," she said.

She took a deep breath, gave the house a final look, and then answered the call.

***

Lauren Wickline opened her eyes and saw only darkness. She blinked rapidly, pushing panic away as she realized the darkness was natural—just the absence of light and not blindness. The last thing she remembered was a fist coming fast toward her. And now here she was, in the darkness.

She tried crying out but could not. She tried opening her mouth but there was something pressed against it. She experientially flicked her tongue forward and felt some sort of cloth pressed tightly to her lips. She felt something hard beneath her back and realized that she was lying down. She rolled over and got to her knees, then pushed up in an attempt to get to her feet. She made it about halfway before the top of her head struck something hard. It made her fall back down and she barely saved her face by throwing her arm out at the last minute.

I've been kidnapped, she thought almost absently. *I knew I should have stayed away from this part of town...Damn it, Lauren, what were you thinking?*

She could barely remember the face of the man at the door but she could remember feeling uneasy when he'd spoken to her. He'd attacked her and now here she was, captured and in some dark confined space that smelled like dust and dirt.

She told herself not to panic, not to start crying, but the tears were already there. As they came, another thought came to her.

He must have knocked me out. And if that's the case, something must have stirred me up out of the darkness. I must have heard something. I must have—

And then she heard a woman's voice. Lauren couldn't make out any words, just slight murmuring. And then she remembered...like coming out of a thick sleep and trying to cling to the last remnants of a dream. The thing that had woken her up. It had been a woman's voice. A fragile voice.

"One minute..."

That's what she had heard. Someone had been shouting it. Someone close by.

In the dark, Lauren began to whine. Through the cloth that was tied around her face, it sounded almost like air escaping from a balloon. She tried to loosen the gag but it was too tight in her mouth, and the knot was small and tight and she couldn't get her fingers to work against it. She looked through the darkness, her cries growing louder as she did her best not to surrender to the panic that was swelling up inside. Ahead of her, she could see the faintest little sliver of light. She crawled toward it, whining through the cloth. As she scrawled, she began to make more sense of the floor beneath her. It felt like unpolished wood. Here and there she also felt strips of dirt. It made her think that she was inside some sort of unfinished structure. But feeling the dirt, she imagined herself in a cellar where there were spiders and snakes in the corners, maybe creeping closer and closer to her.

She reached the sliver of light and saw that it was nothing more than a small amount of light being revealed through a small door. She fumbled at the door, looking for a handle, but there was none.

She slammed her hands against the door, feeling the same sort of wooden surface that was beneath her knees. She shouted as much as she could against the gag on her mouth. Her own muffled shouts rattled in her head but even in the enclosed darkness, she knew that it was not going to sound very loud to anyone on the other side of the door.

She paused and listened, again hearing the muffled sound of a woman speaking. It was still muffled but then a second woman responded. This woman was closer, her voice clearer and decipherable.

"Then again, I'm usually back in my bedroom. I've been bedridden for a few weeks now."

Lauren thought she could imagine what was happening. Someone had knocked on the front door. The woman closest to her had said *One minute!* Now that woman was speaking with another woman. And maybe, Lauren dared hope, the other woman was here, looking for her. Maybe she could help.

Lauren slammed at the door until her hands stung. She felt one of her knuckles split open, blood flowing right away. She stopped banging when she realized it was doing no good. She backed up and turned herself around so that her feet were against the small door. She then drew her feet back and started kicking at the door like she was riding a bike—one foot after another after another.

There was no give to the door and she could barely even sense it buckling and shifting within its frame. She tried shouting again with one final kick that made her knee ache.

When she was done, she listened for the conversation of the two women.

But she fell into despair as she realized they had gone quiet.

CHAPTER THIRTY

"Are you *trying* to get yourself kicked out of the Bureau?" Bryers bellowed into the phone.

Mackenzie hadn't heard Bryers this angry before. Somehow, it was worse than hearing McGrath's voice of rage. Maybe it was because Bryers had gone to bat for her like no one else had before and she felt like she had let him down.

"You said yourself," Mackenzie argued, "that I had been placed into an impossible situation. I'm just trying to make it a little more manageable."

"I am not your boss." Bryers said, "but I am going to tell you right now that if you don't have your ass back home within the hour, you're going to be in a world of trouble. What the hell did you expect to do, anyway? Just hunt the guy down on your own?"

"No, I—"

"This whole time I thought the Scarecrow Killer praise had slid right off your back. But it seems it's all gone to your head, hasn't it? You're not invincible, White. And maybe you're not as good as everyone keeps telling you...you're certainly not as *smart* as I thought you were."

"Are you done, Bryers?"

He gave an exasperated laugh. "No, I'm good. I'm afraid it might be you that's done, White. And I hate to do this, but if you don't give me your express word *right now* that you're going back home, I'm going to report you."

"Fine," Mackenzie said, not caring that she sounded like a spoiled child. "I'll head to the car right now and if the killer is here and we give him a few more hours to land another victim, then what?"

"That's not for you to worry about," Bryers said.

Mackenzie was so frustrated with the answer that she hung up on him. She pocketed her phone and although it sickened her to do so, she turned to head back for her car. She disagreed with his mindset but she knew that he was right. She was not only putting herself in potential danger, she was basically going out of her way to disobey a supervisor that was doing whatever he could to make sure she didn't get expelled.

She made her way back down Estes Street. When she was about to cross over to Sawyer, which would lead her to her car on Black Mill Street, she stopped to let a turning truck pass by. The driver gave her a cursory glance, a stare that was on the verge of checking her out in a sexual way. She rolled her eyes at him, watched the truck pass by, and then crossed the street.

When she did, a realization struck her like a bullet. Something she had missed moments ago…just before she thought she'd heard the additional thumping noise as the old woman had closed the door.

She thought of the old woman and the very brief conversation they'd had. The woman had claimed to have been in poor health— well, not *poor* health but laid up at least. She'd also gone so far as to say that a healthier diet and lifestyle would do her some good. And she'd been overweight…by quite a bit.

It might not be too much of a stretch to think that she might have called on Dana Moore's Natural Health Remedies for assistance. And if she'd not been feeling well, it might also make sense that she'd called upon Avon…if not to make herself feel better with the often-therapeutic assistance of makeup, but just to keep from leaving the house. Hadn't Becka Rudolph even said something about Dana planning to visit some woman in this area that was overweight?

All of a sudden, that extra thump she thought she'd heard seemed a little more important.

Torn, Mackenzie again found herself at a literal crossroads as she stood at the intersection. She looked back toward the house where the old lady had answered the door. While she certainly hadn't seemed like a killer, there could easily be much more to the situation than she could understand from having spoken to the woman for a total of one minute.

She was already here…and the house was almost within sight from where she stood. Would it *really* make things much worse to postpone taking Bryers's advice for another five minutes?

She stood at the crossroads, torn, staring back at the house. Her future, she knew, was on the line. She could step forward, to safety.

Or back, to getting fired. To being sent back to Nebraska.

Mackenzie took a deep breath and silenced her phone.

She turned around and went back.

CHAPTER THIRTY ONE

When Mackenzie came to the yard, she stopped and examined the side of the house. From the right side, she saw nothing of interest. Just a mostly dead yard and a few long-forgotten pieces of lumber. She walked as casually as she could along the street until she got to the left side of the house. There, she saw what appeared to be an addition to the house that had been built on as an afterthought. It was made of plywood and had cheap-looking vinyl siding covering most of it.

From what she could tell, there were no windows on the addition. A single door sat in the wall to the left. A set of concrete stairs sat crooked on the ground below it. While the structure gave her no real cause for concern, she did find it odd and almost out of place. She also noticed that the bottom of the add-on was layered in a series of boards and what looked like some cheap sort of sealant that had been painted over with black paint.

She thought about calling Bryers to report this but knew that it would only invite him to get angrier with her. She was already stepping into the fire. It made no sense to help Bryers and McGrath stoke the coals.

Mackenzie looked away from the eyesore of the add-on and to the house's front door. She supposed she could knock again and ask to come in so she could ask some more questions. But if there *was* something going on here, knocking would give away the element of surprise. The unfortunate run-down from the house on Black Mill Street was proof of that.

More aware than ever that she was completely unarmed, Mackenzie steeled up her courage and walked into the yard. She kept her eyes on the house, making sure no one was looking out at her through the windows or coming out of the front door. She slunk around toward the back yard, her eyes fixed on the back side of the house where the ugly addition that had been built on seemed to call to her.

***

His ma was out of her room. He guessed she was just hungry. It *was* dinner time and the only time she willingly came out of her dungeon of a room was to shove more food into her face. She was sitting on the couch when he walked in, giving him a thoughtful look.

"I'll start on dinner in a second," he said. He walked into the kitchen and set the bag he had brought in from the truck down on the table. When he'd put the teenage girl in the crawlspace, he'd realized that the gag he used was fraying. So he'd gone down to Wal-mart and picked up a few cheap scarves.

"You're not my slave, Jim," she said. "I can make my own dinner."

"The last time you tried making dinner, you burned everything and the smoke alarms went off," Jim said. "It's okay. I'll make it."

"Okay," she said absently.

This was the relationship they had. At some point during her fall in health and his realization that a life of love and marriage and socializing with other people was not for him, their roles had switched. She was very much the child now and Jim was the resentful parent that wished like hell things could be different.

As he pulled a box of spaghetti noodles from the cupboard, she called out to him from the living room. "Did you see any police cars on your way in?" she asked.

"No," he said, his heart instantly blaring an alarm that seemed to pulse in his head. "Why would you ask that?"

"Some lady came by, said she was with the FBI," Ma said. "She said they were looking for a fugitive that was on the run or something."

He dropped the unopened box of noodles on the counter and walked quickly into the living room. "How long ago was this?" he asked.

She shrugged, as if she really didn't care. "Five minutes ago?" she said. "Maybe ten?"

Jim thought about the woman he had seen on the street when he had turned off of Sawyer and onto Estes Street. He'd thought she looked out of place, almost like she was lost. He'd even grinned to himself when he wondered if she might be trying to sell something door to door.

"Is something wrong?" Ma asked him.

He dashed to the couch and spread the curtains open. The yard was empty, as was the street in front of the house (with the exception of his truck). There was so sign of the woman that he had passed—or any other people, for that matter.

Paranoid, he thought. *This is a bad part of town. There's about a thousand reasons the FBI might be in the area.*

He wanted to believe that, but something felt…wrong.

He tried to ignore it. He went into the kitchen and started boiling a pot of water for the spaghetti. But before the first of the bubble started to rise, a pit of worry started to form in his stomach. He stood there motionlessly, holding a frying pan from the cupboard.

He looked into the living room. His mother was looking through a magazine, zoned out.

"I'll be right back," he said, gripping the frying pan.

He felt sick all of a sudden. But under the broiling in his gut and the pressure in his head, there was also a sense of excitement. It was similar to the way he felt when he strangled the people he captured. It was that feeling that pushed him on through the back of his mother's house and to his small addition.

CHAPTER THIRTY TWO

Mackenzie approached the door and was not at all surprised to find it locked. The door itself was flimsy, made of a very cheap and hollow wood. When she rattled at the knob, the door shook slightly in its frame. She thought long and hard about simply kicking it down. One or two swift kicks would do the job.

If she'd had a weapon, she might have done that. She stepped away from the door and looked around the place. She went to the back of the building and saw more scattered lumber. Most of it was mildewed and rotten, having sat discarded ever since the addition had been made. She quietly hunted through the wood and found a solid portion of a two-by-four near the bottom. As she did so, the top of the pile slid off and clattered against the back side of the building.

The thudding noise the wood made against the exterior wall was eerily familiar.

Mackenzie dropped to her knees and lightly rapped at the boards. As she did, she thought of the scratch they had seen on Trevor Simms's head and the discussion about a cage or containment unit of some kind.

Or maybe some sort of crawlspace, Mackenzie thought, looking at the sloppy construction along the bottom of the building. With the sealant and the way it had been painted over, it was almost as if someone was trying to make *just* the bottom part of the building more secure than the rest.

She knocked harder this time, the sound of her knuckles muted against the painted-over sealant and boards. The sound was flat and yielded nothing.

But she got a response this time—a noise that sent a jolt of electricity through her heart.

It was a strangled scream—a woman, from the sound of it.

Grabbing up the two-by-four, Mackenzie got to her feet and turned to the right, making the decision to kick the door down.

And then she saw the man standing there—just a second too late.

*

She wasn't sure what he held in his hand but whatever it was, it was rushing at her head, guided by his fist. There was a loud *clang* as it connected with her face.

144

A frying pan, she thought dimly as sharp pain embraced the right side of her head. *Did he really just hit me with a fry—*

For a moment, Mackenzie saw a black curtain fall over her sight as she fell to the ground. She scrambled to get back up but the man was already on her and pinning her to the ground.

His face was familiar. It was the man from the truck. And he was big—indicative of the large hands that were even now wrapping around her throat and squeezing with deadly pressure.

CHAPTER THIRTY THREE

Within just a few seconds, Mackenzie became less worried about being strangled to death and more worried about having her neck broken. The black curtain that had flickered in her sight moments ago had now become dark flares that seemed to explode like fireworks. The face of the man above her was becoming blurry and her lungs were fighting overtime to draw in a breath.

She grasped frantically at the ground, looking for anything that might help her fight back. As she grasped for something, the fingernail on her ring finger bent backwards but the pain was minuscule compared to the horrendous vise grip the man had on her neck. She fought beneath him but not too much; she knew that she'd expel all of her energy by doing so—energy she would need to put as much force behind an attack whenever the right opportunity presented itself.

Her hands still in search of a weapon, she felt the edge of the two-by-four she'd been holding before being attacked. She pulled it to her, gripped it tightly, and then drew up all of the strength remaining in her body. She brought the two-by-four up as hard as she could, blessed that she'd found it with her right hand instead of her much weaker left.

The board caught the man in the side of the head. He seemed more surprised than hurt but that was fine. His grip on her neck eased up and his bewilderment lasted about two seconds—long enough for her to bring the board up again. She did so at an angle this time and it smashed into his cheek and nose. She was pretty sure the cracking noise she'd heard was his nose breaking, not the board.

He tottered over, trying to keep his balance. Mackenzie grabbed his arms and shoved him hard. That threw his balance off and he went sprawling against the side of the building. Mackenzie tried scrambling to her feet but her legs felt like rubber. She was coughing as she drew air in, her neck feeling like it was already swelling from the inside and black dots of pain and panic blinking in and out in front of her eyes.

She hefted herself up with the help of the board and felt a stinging in her palms. She looked down and was dimly aware that there were two crooked and rusty nails sticking out of the wood. They had sliced into the meat of her palm, drawing pin pricks of blood. She switched ends and hobbled over to the man. He was getting slowly to his feet, his hand covering his nose as blood rushed out. Blood was trailing down his face. His eyes looked both hurt and furious.

Before he made it to his feet, Mackenzie took a rushing stride toward him. She brought her right knee up, connecting solidly under his chin. There was a sharp clicking noise as his teeth snapped together. His eyes flickered dreamily as he leaned slowly back and then fell to the ground in a heap.

She was pretty sure she had knocked him out but didn't want to waste time finding out. Her legs still regaining strength, Mackenzie ran to the concrete steps of the built-on addition. She drew her right leg back and kicked as hard as she could. She missed the doorknob by about three inches, but the cheap door still buckled from the inside. A hinge and substandard lock still held it in place, though. Still coughing to draw air into her sore neck, she reared back and threw her shoulder into it.

The door went sailing inward as it popped off of the hinges. Mackenzie went falling with it, skidding across the floor in an almost comical way along the top of the door. As she scrambled to her feet, she took stock of the place.

She was in a very small central area. An untidy bedroom sat in front of her, about the size of a college dorm room. To her right was a collection of old milk crates filled with magazines and assorted papers. To her left, there was a small door. It was roughly three feet tall and two feet wide. It was made of some sort of metal, much stronger than the meager plywood walls around it. A simple U-shaped handle served as the knob.

The door was locked from the outside by a simple hooking mechanism, but it was a large one—not the small kind that could often be found on screen doors, but the large industrial kind that was used on the tailgates of work trucks. It was hooked into a rugged-looking steel plate on the small door frame.

Realizing that she still had the two-by-four gripped in her hand, she let it drop to the floor. She went to her knees, her hand grasping the large iron hook. It took some strength, but she was able to free it from the latch. She then opened the door, trying her best to prepare herself for what she might see on the other side.

At first, she saw only darkness. But at the very first second, she could feel something stirring inside, shifting around the hot and dusty air that revealed itself when the door was opened. She saw right away that she was looking into a crawlspace. Portions of a badly made wooden floor covered most of it, but there were sections where the dirt floor was also revealed.

147

Mackenzie peered inside, wetting her tongue and trying to push the word *Hello* through her aching neck.

That's when a ghostlike face suddenly seemed to rocket out of the darkness toward her. Of course, as Mackenzie stumbled back in shock, she realized that it was simply a person—a young girl—crawling toward her out of the farthest corners of the darkness.

The girl had a gag around her mouth and a bruise along the left side of her head. Her eyes were glazed and full of fear. She mumbled something through the gag and Mackenzie could tell that the girl was just one slight push away from sliding into utter and uncontrollable panic.

"It's okay," Mackenzie said, the words coming out of throat like gravel. "I'm here to help. Can you crawl out of there?"

The girl nodded, her eyes still large and terrified. Mackenzie reached her hand into the darkness for the girl. Their fingers touched and Mackenzie interlocked them.

Something creaked behind her.

She let go of the girl's fingers and turned. The man was coming at her, launching himself through the broken doorway. He was stumbling a bit, still shaken by the knee to the chin, so he was slow and awkward as he lunged at her. Mackenzie took advantage of this, thinking she'd have just enough time to counterattack.

She grabbed the two-by-four and came up to her knees. She gripped the bottom of it, the two rusted nails sticking out of the top. She brought it around at a hard upward angle. This time, the wood *did* break when it slammed into the side of his face. A small explosion of wood shards sprinkled down into her face as she fell back against the wall with the force of her swing.

The man's response was instant. He went to the ground, howling in pain. His feet kicked out blindly, either in a weak attempt at retaliation or in response to the pain, Mackenzie wasn't sure. She saw that a chunk of wood about six inches long was attached along the side of his jaw, held in place by the nails having been driven through his flesh.

Mackenzie quickly turned to the opened door to the crawlspace and reached back out for the girl. She was hesitant at first but then came quickly. When she was close enough, Mackenzie wrapped the girl up in her arms and pulled her out.

Behind them, the man continued to wail, his hands finding the chunk of wood affixed to his face.

Mackenzie took the girl's head in her hands and looked her in the eyes. "Listen," she said. "There are concrete stairs just outside that doorway. Sit on them and *stay put.* I'll be out with you in just a minute."

The girl nodded and when she did, Mackenzie undid the gag. The frayed scarf fell to the floor and the girl let out a stifled cry.

"Go," Mackenzie said.

The girl did as she was instructed, stumbling through the doorway and leaving Mackenzie alone with the killer. Because he was still on the ground, Mackenzie didn't have much of a problem securing him. She drew both of his arms behind his back, not really caring if she popped one of his shoulders out of socket.

He actually seemed to give in, going limp once she had his wrists secured behind his back with her spare set of plastic cuffs.

"You do what I say," she told him. "The moment you fight back, I'm going to grab that wood sticking out of your face and drag it upwards really fast. You understand?"

He said nothing, so she applied more pressure to his wrists. His shoulders reared back a bit further than the human body was supposed to bend. He uttered a cry and nodded.

She hauled him to his feet, turned him around, and pushed him two steps toward the still-opened crawlspace. "On your knees," she said.

He shook his head furiously and tried to step back. When he did, Mackenzie gave him a slight push and tripped him. He fell forward and she caught him by the shoulder as he dropped to his knees. She then placed her hand on the fragment of wood that still barely clung to his face. Blood was trickling down, but not as much as she would have suspected from such a grisly injury.

"Get in," she said.

The man whimpered and started inside. When he was halfway in, Mackenzie drew her foot back and delivered a kick to his backside. He went sprawling into the dark and Mackenzie wasted no time slamming the door behind him. She then fastened the hook to the clasp on the doorframe, not realizing until it had fallen into place that she had started crying somewhere along the line.

She shook the tears away and took several deep breaths. As she dug into her pocket for her cell phone, she went out to the stairs with the girl. She sat down with the girl and placed a reassuring arm around her. Behind them, Mackenzie heard the man in the crawlspace start to scream.

"You okay?" Mackenzie asked her.

The girl said nothing. She simply shook her head and then she, too, started to cry. Mackenzie pulled the girl closer to her and used her free hand to pull up Bryers's number. When she placed the phone to her ear and it started to ring, she was suddenly not fearful of the repercussions.

In fact, she was not afraid of much of anything in that moment.

So why are you on the verge of crying again?

She didn't know the answer to that.

But when Bryers answered the phone, that was not a question that seemed important. In fact, when the phone call was over forty-five seconds later, she tossed her phone into the grass, put her head into the girl's shoulder, and cried right along with her—not needing an answer.

CHAPTER THIRTY FOUR

Four days later

Mackenzie was finally able to eat whatever she wanted. For the three days following her rescue of Lauren Wickline, the doctor had told her that she could only eat soft foods like soup, yogurt, and smoothies. While she was glad her neck was mostly healed (just a few bruises and a slight strain along the left side), she really didn't care about the solid foods. She hadn't had much of an appetite ever since slamming that two-by-four into the killer's face.

The killer's name was Jim Parkerson. In an almost undramatic fashion, he had admitted to the deaths of Shanda Elliot, Susan Kellerman, Trevor Simms, and Dana Moore within an hour of being arrested. He even said there were two more no one had ever discovered but refused to give their names or when he had killed them.

Mackenzie only knew these things because Bryers had called to fill her in. He had called several times, in fact. Mostly, he just wanted to make sure she was okay. He wouldn't come out and say so, but he felt guilty for leaving her on Estes Street. He should have stayed behind and made sure she left right behind him. Again, he never said any of this but Mackenzie could tell.

She was checking her e-mail, reading over the updates on the Jim Parkerson case, when someone knocked on her door. *This is it,* she thought, stepping away from her laptop. *This is Bryers or McGrath coming by to give me my official leave.*

When she opened the door, though, it was neither of them. Instead, it was Harry. He gave her a thin smile that made her feel surprisingly happy.

"How are you?" he asked.

"Sore throat," she said, returning his small smile. "Come in, Harry."

He did, looking around the place like a nervous teenager that was stepping foot into a girl's room for the first time.

"I heard about what happened," Harry said. "Hell, I think *everyone* has heard by now."

"Is it bad?" she asked.

"Not at all. The jealousy everyone had toward you when you came in...it's sort of turned to awe. You're now a certified badass."

She sat down on the couch. "I don't feel like it," she said. "I feel like an absolute wreck."

"You don't look like it, if that helps."

"It does a little," she said with a slight smile.

"So…is there anything I can do for you?" he asked.

She felt like she was being driven by some alien force when she reached her hand out to him. He took it and she gently led him to the couch. He took a seat next to her and before he was settled, she leaned over and kissed him. There was no heat to it, just a small unwavering kiss. Their lips never even parted, though the kiss lasted about five seconds.

"What was that for?" Harry asked when she pulled back.

"For me," she said. "For…I don't know."

Harry nodded, still holding her hand. "You're feeling alone in all of this, aren't you?" he asked.

"Yeah," she said. It was hard to admit, but there it was.

"Well, I'm always here if you need me. For a kiss or whatever else you need." He gave her another smile, this one uncertain and nervous.

She opened her mouth to respond but another knock sounded out at the door.

"So much for feeling alone," Harry said sarcastically. "You usually get this many visitors?"

"No, never," she said, confused.

She answered the door and found three men standing on the other side. The faces were all familiar but the feeling that rolled through her guts was not pleasant.

Bryers, McGrath, and Ellington stood there, looking at her. They all wore solemn looks on their faces but after a moment, Bryers flashed her a smile.

"Can we come in?" he asked.

"Sure," she said, opening the door wider.

They walked in, single file behind her. Like Harry before them, they all took a glance around the apartment. McGrath made himself at home first, sitting down in the small armchair opposite the couch. He looked to Harry uncertainly and then sighed.

"Agent Dougan, correct?" McGrath said. "Harry Dougan?"

"Yes, sir."

"I'm going to ask you to leave, please," McGrath said. "We need to speak with Ms. White in private."

Harry nodded, looking to Mackenzie. He gave her a *what are you gonna do* look and got to his feet. For a fleeting moment, he and Ellington gave one another a rather tense stare. When Harry got to the door, he turned back and waved.

"See you around," he said.

"See you," Mackenzie said.

When Harry had closed the door, the room went quiet for a while. Bryers went to the couch and took the spot Harry had recently vacated. Ellington remained on his feet, standing in front of the door.

"This couldn't just be done over the phone?" Mackenzie asked.

"What's that?" McGrath asked.

"I crossed a line," she said. "I more than crossed it, I obliterated it. I disobeyed several direct orders. The writing is on the wall. I get it."

"Yes, you did all of those things," McGrath said. "And I was pissed beyond belief for about two days. But then...well, yes you did all of that. But you also captured a man that confessed to killing at least six people and you saved a seventeen-year-old girl from certain death. Given that, it's hard to stay upset."

"And there's more," Ellington said. His eyes were set on her in a way that made her feel uneasy. When she returned his gaze she saw, for a moment, the man that she'd nearly embarrassed herself for back in Nebraska.

"That's right," McGrath said. "Over the last two days, there have been several meetings concerning your future. At the root of it all was your apparent penchant for disobedience."

"I'm sorry," Mackenzie said. "Like I said, I—"

"No, it's not like that," Bryers said. He was looking to McGrath expectantly.

"I want you to report back to the Academy tomorrow," McGrath said. "As long as your neck allows it. I want you to finish up and I want you to kick ass. I want you at the top of your class. Can you do that?"

"Yes, sir."

"When your time at the Academy is over, the future is up to you."

"How?" she asked.

McGrath looked to Ellington, silently giving him the floor. "There's a new program for the top-ranked agents coming out of the Academy. We're just now getting it off the ground, but we think you'd be a great way to test it."

"What sort of program?" Mackenzie asked.

"We can't tell you that," McGrath said. "Not while you're in the Academy."

She nodded, confused beyond measure but too afraid to question anything.

"You did some damn fine work," McGrath said. "It was reckless and unnecessarily life-threatening, but you got the job done. You did it on your own and without a firearm. It's one of those stories that *would* live in infamy. But...as we said before I re-tasked you to the assignment, you can't get the credit. Officially, you weren't even there."

She nodded, understanding, and not even caring about the credit. All she cared about was that she saved that girl's life. She could still see her grateful look, remember their shared cry, and that was enough.

"Although," Bryers said, "the true story somehow got out among your peers."

"So," McGrath said, getting to his feet, "think it over. Devote yourself to these last few weeks at the Academy and then get in touch with me. This special position is yours if you want it."

With that, McGrath headed back to the door and opened it. He gave a wave and left as if he had been paying a random visit to discuss the weather. Ellington approached her and gave her an awkward hug before he left. Bryers followed behind him and as he reached the doorway, he turned back to her.

"I'm proud of you, White. Damn fine job."

Bryers grinned at her and then closed the door, leaving Mackenzie alone yet again.

And for the first time since leaving Nebraska, she felt good.

COMING SOON!

Book #3 in the Mackenzie White mystery series!

Blake Pierce

Blake Pierce is author of the bestselling RILEY PAGE mystery series, which include the mystery suspense thrillers ONCE GONE (book #1), ONCE TAKEN (book #2), ONCE CRAVED (#3), and ONCE LURED (#4). Blake Pierce is also the author of the MACKENZIE WHITE mystery series and the AVERY BLACK mystery series.

An avid reader and lifelong fan of the mystery and thriller genres, Blake loves to hear from you, so please feel free to visit www.blakepierceauthor.com to learn more and stay in touch.

BOOKS BY BLAKE PIERCE

RILEY PAIGE MYSTERY SERIES
ONCE GONE (Book #1)
ONCE TAKEN (Book #2)
ONCE CRAVED (Book #3)
ONCE LURED (Book #4)

MACKENZIE WHITE MYSTERY SERIES
BEFORE HE KILLS (Book #1)
BEFORE HE SEES (Book #2)

AVERY BLACK MYSTERY SERIES
CAUSE TO KILL (Book #1)
CAUSE TO RUN (Book #2)

Printed in Great Britain
by Amazon